C. A Browne

The ethnography of the Mullet, Inishkea Islands, and Portacloy, County Mayo : a paper read before the Royal Irish Academy,

February 25, 1895

C. A Browne

The ethnography of the Mullet, Inishkea Islands, and Portacloy, County Mayo : a paper read before the Royal Irish Academy, February 25, 1895

ISBN/EAN: 9783742833860

Manufactured in Europe, USA, Canada, Australia, Japa

Cover: Foto ©Andreas Hilbeck / pixelio.de

Manufactured and distributed by brebook publishing software (www.brebook.com)

C. A Browne

The ethnography of the Mullet, Inishkea Islands, and Portacloy, County Mayo : a paper read before the Royal Irish Academy, February 25, 1895

THE ETHNOGRAPHY

OF

THE MULLET, INISHKEA ISLANDS,

AND

PORTACLOY,

COUNTY MAYO.

BY

CHARLES R. BROWNE, M.D., M.R.I.A.

(PLATES XV., XVI., and XVII.)

A PAPER

Read before the **ROYAL IRISH ACADEMY**, February 25, 1895;

and

Reprinted from the "PROCEEDINGS." 3rd Ser.. Vol. III., No. 4.

[*Fifty copies only reprinted by the Academy for the Author.*]

DUBLIN:

PRINTED AT THE UNIVERSITY PRESS,

BY PONSONBY AND WELDRICK,

PRINTERS TO THE ACADEMY.

1895.

XXXVII.

THE ETHNOGRAPHY OF THE MULLET, INISHKEA ISLANDS, AND PORTACLOY, COUNTY MAYO. By CHARLES R. BROWNE M.D., M.R.I.A.

(PLATES XV., XVI., AND XVII.)

[Read FEBRUARY 25, 1895.]

CONTENTS.

I.—INTRODUCTION.

IN continuance of the series of local surveys undertaken by the Dublin Anthropometric Committee and carried out as part of the work of the Anthropological Laboratory of Trinity College, the third of these surveys was made by me last August in the western portion of the barony of Erris, county Mayo. It was at first intended that only the Parish of Kilmore, including the peninsula known as the Mullet (or Erris proper) and the Inishkea Islands should be undertaken, but unusual facilities for working the isolated district of Portacloy presenting themselves, it also was included in the inquiry.

The circumstances under which the work was carried on differed considerably from those experienced on the two previous occasions, the field being wider and the people more scattered ; but the same methods were adhered to as far as possible, and this report has been drawn up on the same lines as its predecessors, in order to facilitate comparison and reference.

<h2 style="text-align:center">II.—PHYSIOGRAPHY.</h2>

The district dealt with in this Paper consists of two distinct localities, one clearly defined, the parish of Kilmore, the other more indefinite in its boundaries, being a tract of wild mountainous country around the little hamlet of Portacloy; both form part of the barony of Erris, in the extreme north-west of the Co. Mayo.

Kilmore includes the Mullet peninsula, the inhabited islands of North and South Inishkea, Duvillaun and Eagle Island, and a considerable number of uninhabited islets, the most remarkable of which is Inisglora (Inis Gluaire). The Mullet, or Erris proper, is a long narrow strip of land, nearly cut off from the mainland, as it is bounded on the east or landward side by Broadhaven and the magnificent Bay of Blacksod, some forty-five square miles in area, the only connection with the rest of Erris being by a narrow isthmus, about 200 yards in width. The peninsula runs nearly north and south; its extreme length is about fifteen miles, and its width varies from about seven miles in the northern part to less than half a mile near its southern extremity. The total area of the parish, including the islands, is 29,492 acres, or about 46 square miles.

The coast line, in the northern portion, consists mainly of high cliffs, indented by deep coves with precipitous and often overhanging walls, and in places pierced by caves and natural bridges. This precipitous coast extends from Broadhaven, on the north-east, round to Annagh Head on the west, a distance, following the coast line, of about thirty miles, the cliffs rising in many places to above 300 feet, and affording only three inlets of any size. Blind Harbour, on the north (200 acres in area, nearly all dry at low water), and Frenchport and Scotchport on the west, the others are either inaccessible from the land side or only practicable for curraghs. Erris Head forms the extreme north point of the peninsula. Off this part of the coast lies Eagle Island, high and rocky in coast and surface, and a lighthouse-station. From Frenchport (or rather Annagh Head, its southern boundary) southward, the coast is sandy beach, shingle, and low rocks, and is backed to a large extent by rolling ranges of sandhills. Off this part of the coast lie Iniskea and Duvillaun, having a sandy or rocky shore, and a surface of no great elevation. The eastern shore along Blacksod Bay and Broadhaven is sheltered and low.

The surface of the Mullet does not reach any very great elevation, the highest point in the northern part being 410 feet above sea level, and the rounded granite hill of Tarmon, in the extreme south, 369 feet. It is much diversified, a good deal of it being fertile land, especially on the east side, but in the north part there is a good deal of bog and moor, and in the south and west rolling sandhills barely held in check by bent. In some of the narrower portions a fertile belt lies between two sandy ones.

The district of Portacloy is a wild mountainous region, with a coast of precipitous cliffs of great height, and riddled with caves. Benwee Head, which rises above the sea to the height of 1000 feet, is just outside the mouth of the deep narrow inlet which forms the harbour. The surface of this part of the district is very wild, and consists largely of bog and mountain. The climate is very mild, frost and snow being of infrequent occurrence and not lasting for long, but the rains are heavy and almost constant during the greater part of the year, and storms are frequent and severe.

Vegetation flourishes well, but, owing to the storms, trees are very few and only grow in sheltered localities.

The whole district is largely cut off from the outer world by the wide stretch of wild and sparsely peopled country through which the mail road from Ballina runs.[1]

III.—Anthropography.

1. *Methods.*—The methods employed did not differ to any great extent from those made use of on the two previous occasions. A few

---

[1] I am indebted to Mr. G. H. Kinahan, M.R.I.A., for the following note on the geology of the Mullet:—The south rough portion is granite, while the north rough portion is in part Archæan (*query, the equivalent of the Sutherland Algonkian rocks that have been called Old Bay*), and in part of Archæan quartzite (query, the equivalents of the Scotch Torridan Sandstone); while the central portion is occupied by schists of an uncertain age that lie unconformably on the Archæan rock to the northward.

changes were made to bring our observation form into closer accord with that adopted by the Ethnographic Survey Committee of the British Association for use in England. The new form admits of very rapid noting, and in collecting easily and accurately the main physical characters of the persons examined. It has not, however, any advantage over the old form, of which it is a modification, in the convenience of working up results, in fact it is inferior in this respect as the spaces for indices at the bottom of the page, which are omitted, proved a great help in tabulating the results of the Inishbofin Survey ; another defect is that some of the points to be noted are not strictly defined, and leave too much to the personal opinion of the observer.

(A.) *Hair and eye colour.*—No change was made in this part of the work, the method being exactly that used on the two previous occasions. For full particulars the reader is referred to the Report on the visit to the Aran Islands.[1]

(B.) *Measurements and instruments.*—These were the same as formerly employed, with two additions :—(1) *The height of the head* ; and (2) *height of cranium*, both projections, directions for taking which were printed on the observation forms. These measurements were given a trial, as they form part of the series on the English form, but after a time they were abandoned for reasons given below.

The same set of instruments as used in Inishbofin was carried, packed in a canvas case. It consisted of compas d'epaisseur, compas glissière, the portable pattern of Cunningham's craniometer, Garson's anthropometer, steel tape, Snellen test types, note books, nigrescence cards, and observation forms, as before. The only new appliance was a Trinity hand camera, made by Messrs. Curtis, Suffolk-street, Dublin, which, though subjected to rather rough treatment, stood the test admirably and did very satisfactory work. When not in use it was carried in a stout waterproof case slung over the shoulder.

(c). *Remarks on methods employed.*—The work had to be carried on under rather different circumstances from those experienced before, as the weather prevailing during my visit to the district was not too well suited for field work, the rains being frequent and heavy, and the wind very strong, besides this, the population is much more scattered than any dealt with before, and long journeys had often to be made for very little result. In some ways, however, the work

---

[1] Ethnography of the Aran Islands, Co. Galway, Proc. R. I. A., vol. II., 3rd ser., p. 768.

was easier, the measuring being, in many cases, done under shelter, instead of on the hills, the roadside, or the sea-shore.

As is mentioned above the two new measurements had to be abandoned owing to practical difficulties. It is a matter of experience in work of this sort in Ireland that persons do not *come* to be measured, they have to be sought out and induced to submit themselves to the process, often no easy matter; there are generally several to be measured in quick succession, but if kept waiting long they will one by one slip off and refuse to allow measurement; and as the adapting of the anthropometer for these projections takes some time, the instrument having to be unshipped for each, and then fitted up again to measure the next comer, it became evident that these projections would have to be given up if anything like a sufficient number of persons was to be measured. Moreover, accuracy in taking projection measurements is by no means easily obtained, even under the most favourable circumstances in a laboratory, and the difficulty is increased so much in field work, where it is not at all easy to get the men to understand exactly what position they are wanted to assume, so as to make the results unreliable.

The noting of the colours of the hair and eyes also presented some difficulties, the chief being to distinguish between those who were natives and strangers from other districts, which was rendered greater by the absence of a distinctive dress (except in the case of the people of Inishkea). In spite of these difficulties, however, I succeeded in noting the eye and hair colours of 494 individuals, on 62 (male adults) of whom the full series of measurements and observations was made. As on the two former surveys precautions were taken against recording the same person twice, as well as against the inclusion of the men measured in the ordinary nigrescence cards.

(D). *Photography.*—Owing to the rain and rough weather as much could not be done in this department as had been hoped, but in spite of the difficulties of cloudy skies and high winds a number of photographs were taken, including, 17 portraits, 14 of them individuals measured, 12 groups, taken in all parts of the district, 30 illustrations of the occupations, modes of transport, and habitations of the people, also several of the antiquities of the district, and a set of views showing surface of land and nature of coast line, &c.

Some of these photographs were taken by myself, others by my brother J. M. Browne. The addition of the hand camera to our appliances has proved to be a great advantage, enabling portraits of unwilling subjects to be taken, and adding to the value of the photographs of occupations by admitting of their being taken when the performers were in motion. It could also be used on occasions when the high winds would not allow the setting up of a tripod stand.

2.—*Physical Characters* :—

(A). The general physical characters of the people are as given below, though some differences exist between the inhabitants of different parts of the district.

The people on the whole are good-looking, especially when young; many of the girls and young women are very handsome, but they appear to age rapidly and early become wrinkled.

Stature and bulk.—The men of this district are as a rule of fair average stature, very stoutly built, and broad shouldered; while there are few who can fairly be termed very tall, yet many reach a good height, and the proportion of small men is by no means large. The average stature of the 62 adult males measured was 1725 mm., or about 5 feet 8 inches. The extremes were 1628 mm. (5 feet 4 inches), and 1820 mm., or about 5 feet 11½ inches.

The women seem to be more even in height than the men.

Limbs.—The hands are usually of medium size, broad and with fingers squarely clubbed at the ends. The forearms (measured from styloid process to the head of radius) are often very long for the stature, and the span is sometimes very great, though in a few cases it is less than the stature, a character also noted in the Aran Islands, though the proportion of cases in which it was observed was much greater there.

Head.—The head is generally well shaped and is often of large size. The forehead is broad and upright (rarely receding), rounded away at the sides, and of fair height; superciliary ridges and glabella of no great size, eye-brows thick and level.

The cranial curve rises to a pretty fair height above the ears (height index 65·8), though not attaining the altitude seen in the people of Aran and the men of Inishbofin, and descends in an even sweep to the occipital protuberance as the occipital region does not usually project.

In the majority of cases, as will be seen from the table of indices, the head is mesaticephalic, the mean index being 77·4 (when two units are deducted to reduce to the cranial standard). Of the 62 persons measured, 10 were brachycephalic, and 11 dolichocephalic. The extremes were 86·2 and 72·3.

Face.—The face is of medium length, with prominent cheek-bones, and is rather broader in the bigonial region than observed in either Aran or Inishbofin.

The nose is short and has nearly always a straight profile; of the 62 men measured, 50 had straight, 8 sinuous, 2 aquiline, and 2 retroussé noses.

The wrinkles on the face are very deep, most so about the eyes and at the "root" of the nose, where there is often a raised fold of skin between two deep furrows. The mouth is large, with lips of medium thickness, often kept habitually apart when the face is at rest, but the large hanging lower lip is not so noticeable a character here as in other localities of the west coast.

The teeth are usually very short and even.

The chin is prominent, but not long, and the angles of the jaw are rather oblique.

The eyes, which are placed moderately wide apart, have irides of a light blue or bluish-gray, and being deep set and (in the fishermen) habitually half closed, they present to a casual observer the appearance of being small in size.

The ears are small, projecting, and rather coarsely moulded. Abnormalities of the lobule are common, and were seen in 33 out of the 62 men on whom observations were made; of these the lobule was absent in 10, and attached in 23. Absence of the lobule is very common in the northern part of the Mullet, and appears to be a local character there; in nearly all the men seen at Muingerena this part of the organ was either of very small size or was absent altogether. Flattening out of the pinna and Darwinian tubercle were observed in several cases.

Skin.—Wrinkles, as before mentioned, come early, first appearing about the eyes.

The complexion is either ruddy or pale, rarely sallow; on exposure to the sun and wind it becomes a clear red, seldom freckling or turning brown.

Hair.—The prevailing colour for the hair is dark brown, next in order of frequency is brown or chestnut, next black; fair and red hair are comparatively scarce.

In the case of the Inishkea people, the most usual hair colour seems to be a clear brown, accompanied by reddish-brown beard and blue-grey eyes; in these islands also, there is a larger proportion of fair hair than on the mainland. The hair and beard (when worn) are fairly abundant. Greyness does not appear to set in early.

Sight and Hearing.—Both these senses are very acute, especially the former, which, in the fishermen, is extremely keen, many of these men can see small objects floating on the water at a distance where, even by the aid of a strong glass, most persons would find great difficulty in seeing them at all.

This description being a general one, little mention has been made of the differences which exist between the people of different parts of the district. It appears to be the general opinion on the mainland, that the inhabitants of North Inishkea are taller than those of the South Island, and, also, that the natives of both islands are fairer than those of the mainland, and personal inspection has corroborated these opinions. The islanders are readily distinguishable from the mainland people, not only by their dress of blue homespun, but also by their fairer hair and complexion, and their different cast of features.

The men of the district round Portacloy are darker in hair and seem to be of a different type; many of them are exceedingly fine well-built fellows.

In no part of the district are the people of small stature, though a large number of them are descendants of dispossessed Ulster people. On the contrary, they appear to be taller and stouter than the inhabitants of the southern part of the country. A statement,[1] originally made by an anonymous writer, has somehow gained currency, and has been repeatedly quoted abroad, noticeably by M. De Quatrefages,[2] and by M. Devay,[3] that the descendants of the Ulster people driven two centuries ago into Sligo and Mayo, had dwindled into dwarfs of five feet two inches high, prognathous and pot-bellied.

This most certainly does not apply to any section of the inhabitants of this part of Mayo, if indeed it were ever true of any part of the counties named, which repeated inquiries and personal observation agree in denying most positively.

The statement is quite unsupported by other writers dealing with this region at the same time. Thus Mr. P. Knight, writing in 1834, says of the people of Erris that " they are generally a good-humoured, good-natured, hospitable, generous race—*of middle size*— active, intelligent, and, when an opportunity offers of showing it, industrious." C. O.[4] describes the people as tall.

---

[1] Dublin University Magazine, No. 48, p. 658.
[2] L'Unité de l'Espèce Humain, ii., 316.
[3] Devay Fr. " Du Danger des Mariages consanguins sous le Rapport Sanitaire."
[4] " Sketches in Erris and Tyrawley."

CEPHALIC INDICES, CORRECTED FOR COMPARISON WITH SKULLS.

No.	Index.	A. Corrected Indices.
		B. Actual Indices.
41	86.2	
11	85.1	
32	83.4	
15	82.8	
8	82.5	} 10 Brachycephalic.
60	82.5	
54	82.1	
57	81.5	
53	81.3	
31	80.6	} 20 Brachycephals.
61	79.7	
7	79.4	
30	79.1	
43	79.1	
51	79.1	
3	78.5	
13	78.4	
19	78.4	
23	78.0	
34	78.0	
2	77.9	
35	77.9	
36	77.9	
47	77.6	
50	77.6	
28	77.4	
1	77.2	
18	77.0	
26	77.0	
62	77.0	
27	76.9	} 41 Mesaticephalic.
46	76.9	
37	76.8	
16	76.6	
22	76.6	
25	76.5	
24	76.4	
42	76.2	
20	76.1	
44	76.1	} 39 Mesaticephals.
49	76.0	
52	75.9	
33	75.9	
29	75.8	
39	75.8	
58	75.7	
56	75.5	
48	75.3	
38	75.0	
12	75.0	
55	75.0	
4	74.8	
6	74.5	
59	74.4	
40	74.3	
9	74.0	
17	74.0	} 11 Dolichocephalic.
10	73.5	
14	73.5	
45	72.7	
21	72.5	} 3 Dolichocephals.
5	72.3	

(B.) *Statistics of Eye and Hair Colours :—*

ADULTS.—I. *Males.*

HAIR.		Light.	Medium.	Dark.	Totals.	Percentage Hair Colours.
			EYES.			
Red,	..	4	1	—	5	2.43
Fair,	..	14	—	—	14	6·79
Brown,	..	74	7	2	83	40·29
Dark,	..	79	6	3	88	42·72
Black,	..	8	5	3	16	7·77
Totals,	..	179	19	8	206	100·00
Percentage Eye Colours, }		86·89	9·22	3·89	100·00	—

Index of Nigrescence, . . 49·04.

ADULTS.—II. *Females.*

HAIR.		Light.	Medium.	Dark.	Totals.	Percentage Hair Colours.
			EYES.			
Red,	..	5	—	—	5	3·47
Fair,	..	2	—	—	2	1·39
Brown,	..	52	2	4	58	40·28
Dark,	..	33	21	12	66	45·83
Black,	..	7	2	4	13	9·03
Totals,	..	99	25	20	144	100·00
Percentage Eye Colours, }		68·75	17·36	13·89	100·00	—

Index of Nigrescence, . . . 59·03.
Combined Index (both sexes), . 54·03.

CHILDREN.—I. *Boys.*

HAIR.	EYES.			Totals.	Percentage Hair Colours.
	Light.	Medium.	Dark.		
Red, ..	4	—	—	4	5·40
Fair, ..	10	—	—	10	13·51
Brown, ..	34	—	—	34	45·95
Dark, ..	23	1	—	24	32·43
Black. ..	2	—	—	2	2·71
Totals, ..	73	1	—	74	100·00
Percentage Eye Colours, }	98·65	1·35	—	100·00	—

Index of Nigrescence, . . 18·94.

CHILDREN.—II. *Girls.*

HAIR.	EYES.			Totals.	Percentage Hair Colours.
	Light.	Medium.	Dark.		
Red, ..	—	—	—	—	—
Fair, ..	10	—	—	10	15·87
Brown, ..	29	1	—	30	47·62
Dark, ..	16	2	4	22	34·92
Black, ..	1	—	—	1	1·59
Totals, ..	56	3	4	63	100·00
Percentage Eye Colours, }	88·89	4·76	6·35	100·00	—

Index of Nigrescence, ... 23·23.
Combined Index (both sexes), . 21·09.

TOTAL.—I. *Males.*

| HAIR. | EYES. | | | Totals. | Percentage Hair Colours. |
	Light.	Medium.	Dark.		
Red, ..	8	1	—	9	3·21
Fair, ..	24	—	—	24	8·57
Brown, ..	108	7	2	117	41·79
Dark, ..	102	7	3	112	40·00
Black, ..	10	5	3	18	6·43
Totals, ..	252	20	8	280	100·00
Percentage Eye Colours, }	90·0	7·14	2·86	100·00	—

Index of Nigrescence, . . 41·08.

TOTAL.—II. *Females.*

| HAIR. | EYES. | | | Totals. | Percentage Hair Colours. |
	Light.	Medium.	Dark.		
Red, ..	5	—	—	· 5	2·41
Fair, ..	12	—	—	12	5·79
Brown, ..	81	3	4	88	42·52
Dark, ..	49	23	16	88	42·52
Black, ..	8	2	4	14	6·76
Totals, ..	155	28	24	207	100·00
Percentage Eye Colours, }	74·88	13·53	11·59	100·00	—

Index of Nigrescence, . . . 47·84.
Combined Index (both sexes), . 44·46.

(c.) *Physical Proportions.*—As in foregoing reports, the proportions borne by the main measurements to the stature (taken as 100) have been calculated, and are given in this paper: they differ considerably from those of the people of the districts previously visited.

Face.

The face is not so long in proportion as met with in either of the other localities. It varies between 6·48 and 8·26, with a mean of 7·36: it is over 8 in one instance, and below 7 in nine out of the sixty-two recorded.

Upper Face.—Mean 4·30, as compared with 4·42 for Inishbofin.

Nose.—This is not very constant in its relation to body-height, having a mean of 3·10 and extremes of 2·65 and 3·98. Thus, on the whole, this feature is much shorter in the Erris people than in the Aran Islanders (3·38) or the natives of Inishbofin, in whom the mean exactly equalled the canon (3·30).

Sitting Height.

This measurement was for the first time taken regularly in field-work in this district. The mean of the series is 51·33, but it varies in individual cases between 49·44 and 55·29.

Upper Limb.

Span.—Several cases are recorded in this series in which this measurement falls short of the stature, a character found to be common in the Aran Islands, where it was met with in more than one-fourth of those measured. The proportion in this case is one in fifteen. Of the four cases, three are from North Inishkea and one from the Mullet. The mean occupies a position between that of Aran and that of Inishbofin, being 104·36 as against 101·94 and 104·95.

Hand.—This member is rather short, and is, as a rule, fairly constant in its proportion to stature. It ranges, however, in extreme cases between 10·10 and 12·24, and averages 11·34, being thus the same as the mean of Inishbofin (11·33).

Forearm.—The forearm is long, giving a mean of 15·43, very much greater than is the case either in the Aran series (15·18) or in that of Inishbofin (15·03).

(D.) *Detailed List of Measurements:—*

No.	INDICES.						PROPORTIONS TO STATURE.—HEIGHT = 100.						
	Cephalic.	Height.	Facial.	Bigonial.	Alveolar.	Nasal.	Hand.	Forearm.	Span.	Height Sitting.	Face.	Upper Face.	Nose.
1	79·2	64·4	115·6	92·2	98·0	66·7	10·99	14·70	105·92	52·73	7·21	4·06	3·04
2	79·9	63·3	123·3	91·7	95·1	64·2	10·88	14·71	101·76	53·65	7·06	3·88	3·12
3	80·5	66·7	100·0	85·5	97·9	63·3	10·10	15·29	100·06	53·93	7·75	4·38	3·37
4	76·8	63·1	103·0	81·8	97·9	63·0	10·91	14·98	97·41	52·77	7·78	4·48	3·18
5	74·3	62·9	104·5	88·1	102·1	60·0	11·38	15·65	104·15	51·68	7·63	4·44	3·42
6	76·5	61·8	93·9	78·2	101·0	56·7	11·57	15·45	104·78	49·44	8·26	4·38	3·37
7	81·4	64·4	104·6	87·7	100·0	68·0	11·24	14·78	101·71	53·34	7·69	4·43	2·95
8	84·5	66·8	103·7	80·1	92·6	65·4	10·59	15·03	99·94	54·10	7·70	4·30	2·94
9	76·0	63·0	111·7	85·0	100·0	57·1	11·11	14·62	103·10	52·63	7·02	4·21	3·27
10	75·5	65·0	123·6	94·5	102·1	68·8	10·55	15·85	98·23	51·95	6·71	4·16	2·92
11	87·1	69·4	115·0	86·7	97·8	62·1	10·60	14·40	101·29	53·51	7·03	4·21	3·40
12	77·0	65·0	111·1	87·3	100·0	84·3	12·02	14·42	108·77	51·56	7·57	4·03	3·43
13	80·4	65·2	105·6	84·9	95·8	45·5	11·87	15·72	107·23	51·51	7·59	4·88	3·98
14	75·5	64·3	103·9	71·9	101·1	62·6	11·95	15·42	101·14	52·08	7·63	4·67	3·24
15	84·8	67·0	115·6	89·1	98·9	57·6	11·35	15·10	—	52·50	7·26	4·26	3·35
16	78·6	64·8	113·5	88·9	106·0	73·1	11·65	14·99	105·09	54·33	7·38	4·51	3·04
17	76·0	62·5	109·7	89·6	110·3	65·4	11·26	16·86	104·85	51·10	7·74	4·68	3·18
18	79·0	67·5	105·3	83·2	106·2	60·0	11·49	15·63	102·71	52·66	7·41	4·19	3·11
19	80·4	64·9	98·7	79·4	105·3	58·2	11·11	15·76	100·51	51·81	7·97	4·46	3·11
20	78·1	67·3	104·5	82·4	105·3	56·1	11·65	14·84	100·25	50·72	7·20	4·01	2·80
21	74·5	62·5	111·5	94·3	108·3	55·5	11·55	16·72	104·06	53·45	7·08	4·59	3·13
22	78·6	65·3	113·8	86·2	99·0	73·5	11·89	15·79	108·97	52·74	7·58	4·43	2·86
23	80·0	66·5	111·9	87·3	102·1	74·5	11·41	16·55	104·12	53·47	7·53	4·55	3·05
24	78·4	64·8	103·7	91·9	97·9	52·7	11·74	16·95	105·22	56·43	8·00	4·62	3·26
25	78·5	67·0	115·0	95·6	102·1	61·1	11·47	15·09	104·42	50·89	6·48	3·84	3·10
26	79·0	68·2	110·7	91·0	105·4	64·7	11·16	14·72	102·26	53·71	7·24	4·39	3·03
27	78·9	65·8	115·8	93·0	98·9	59·6	11·61	15·79	109·21	54·05	7·00	4·73	3·50
28	79·4	65·5	103·2	86·5	101·1	54·5	11·35	15·70	100·65	51·73	7·41	4·47	3·29

29	2·91	4·23	6·98	51·65	101·68	14·89	10·88	56·6	97·8	82·7	111·8	67·0	77·8
30	3·00	3·96	7·07	53·48	104·30	15·28	11·71	58·5	104·5	96·8	115·2	65·8	81·1
31	3·34	4·22	7·73	53·90	103·98	15·29	11·42	57·1	102·1	84·8	103·8	65·8	82·6
32	3·07	4·00	6·60	53·48	104·29	15·06	11·82	62·3	95·8	98·2	122·8	68·5	85·4
33	3·25	4·38	7·17	54·43	108·31	15·54	11·94	53·4	102·0	85·6	107·6	64·8	77·9
34	2·86	3·97	6·66	55·29	109·88	15·25	11·69	69·4	110·2	96·5	128·1	66·5	80·0
35	2·87	4·21	7·02	54·43	102·40	15·04	10·59	61·2	98·9	92·6	110·0	66·1	79·9
36	3·12	4·45	7·69	52·20	106·24	16·53	10·86	66·7	108·2	76·7	104·5	64·4	79·9
37	2·96	4·27	6·88	54·14	111·49	15·53	11·26	61·5	92·7	100·0	115·7	65·5	78·8
38	3·17	4·37	7·60	53·85	105·44	15·31	11·11	71·4	107·9	88·0	106·7	63·5	77·0
39	3·15	4·28	6·93	53·21	108·11	14·98	11·77	60·7	103·3	87·8	113·0	66·2	77·8
40	3·16	4·16	7·30	53·91	102·66	14·52	10·64	66·7	97·9	83·3	113·6	68·7	76·3
41	3·12	4·28	7·23	53·58	105·78	15·26	10·13	61·1	90·5	83·2	118·4	71·6	88·2
42	3·06	4·22	6·94	52·20	99·31	15·20	11·16	67·9	100·0	100·0	120·8	64·5	78·2
43	2·93	4·30	7·29	53·64	103·17	15·05	11·23	68·0	104·2	93·4	120·5	67·3	81·1
44	2·93	4·63	7·62	55·18	102·32	15·61	11·71	72·9	102·1	92·8	112·8	61·8	78·1
45	3·27	4·36	7·22	52·76	104·47	15·65	11·30	61·4	100·0	88·0	110·4	65·7	74·7
46	3·20	4·18	7·26	53·52	105·17	14·53	11·85	72·7	106·1	85·7	113·5	64·7	78·9
47	3·09	4·45	7·25	51·99	108·50	16·16	11·35	61·5	99·0	90·3	111·3	64·3	79·6
48	3·14	4·05	6·96	52·74	106·51	15·70	11·41	60·0	96·1	90·2	115·0	68·6	77·3
49	3·04	4·35	7·27	54·42	105·96	15·69	11·05	66·0	101·0	93·6	118·3	66·0	78·0
50	2·80	3·97	7·33	52·85	104·59	15·04	11·07	66·0	103·8	95·4	117·6	67·0	79·6
51	2·90	4·32	7·00	51·89	105·62	14·44	11·66	75·5	100·0	94·1	115·9	63·8	81·1
52	2·90	4·46	7·71	52·75	104·64	15·07	11·59	62·1	99·9	88·7	109·8	67·3	77·9
53	3·34	4·48	8·00	50·90	104·36	16·30	12·24	66·0	100·0	81·8	104·5	65·6	83·3
54	3·21	3·71	6·48	50·68	104·60	15·62	11·96	73·3	101·1	100·1	129·1	68·7	84·1
55	2·65	3·96	7·27	51·73	106·38	15·54	11·41	77·1	94·7	95·9	118·7	65·2	77·0
56	2·84	3·98	7·24	53·20	110·00	16·46	11·33	74·0	100·0	96·2	109·9	64·2	77·5
57	2·71	4·36	6·99	52·84	108·41	16·12	11·64	62·3	97·1	97·4	123·1	68·6	83·5
58	3·16	4·08	7·13	52·68	103·53	15·41	11·08	72·9	101·0	102·6	122·2	62·4	77·7
59	2·92	4·51	7·85	53·02	104·57	15·29	11·13	65·4	100·0	85·8	104·5	65·9	76·4
60	3·05	4·12	7·25	51·28	101·52	15·94	10·87	55·3	102·1	91·0	107·7	68·0	84·5
61	3·12	4·54	7·31	53·21	101·36	15·91	11·26	57·9	100·0	91·1	112·9	70·2	81·7
62	3·36	4·39	7·57	54·26	104·52	15·85	11·33	73·6	100·0	91·5	112·4	66·7	79·0
[enm.]	3·10	4·30	7·36	51·33	104·36	15·43	11·34	64·0	100·6	89·3	111·9	65·8	79·4

No.	Name.	Age.	Locality.	Eye Colour.	Hair Colour.	Skin.	Ears.	CEPH. Length.
1	Lavelle, Philip, .	33	Inishkea, N.	blue	dark-brown	ruddy	Outstanding, lobes attached	202
2	Lavelle, William,	38	Inishkea, N.	light-grey	brown	ruddy	Outstanding, lobes attached	199
3	Cawley, Patrick,	40	Inishkea, S.	light-grey	dark	ruddy	Lobes attached	210
4	Cawley, Michael,	41	Inishkea, S.	blue	brown	ruddy	Outstanding, lobes absent	198
5	Lavelle, Michael,	32	Inishkea, N.	blue	light-brown	ruddy	Flat, lobes detached	202
6	Lavelle, William,	27	Inishkea, N.	dark-grey	black	pale	Outstanding, lobes detached	204
7	Reilly, Michael, .	32	Inishkea, N.	blue	fair	ruddy	Flat, lobes attached	194
8	Reilly, John, . .	28	Inishkea, N.	blue	brown	ruddy	Outstanding	193
9	Lavelle, Patrick, .	28	Inishkea, N.	blue	brown	ruddy	Outstanding	200
10	Lavelle, John, .	31	Inishkea, N.	blue	brown	ruddy	—	200
11	O'Reilly, P. T.,	17	Carne, Mullet	dark-grey	dark	pale	Flat	186
12	Gaughan, Wm., .	28	Emlybeg, Mullet	dark-grey	dark	freckled	Flat, lobes absent	200
13	Dunlevy, Anth., .	60	Emlybeg, Mullet	blue	brown	ruddy	Outstanding, lobes attached	184
14	Gaughan, Michl.,	60	Moyrahan, Mullet	blue	black	ruddy	Outstanding	196
15	Clery, Francis, .	22	Belmullet	dark-grey	black	ruddy	Outstanding, lobes attached	191
16	Coyle, William, .	28	Shanaghy	light-brown	black	dark	Outstanding	196
17	Geraghty, Michl.,	30	Mullaghroe	blue	dark	ruddy	Outstanding, lobes attached	200
18	Cawley, Patrick,	58	Aughleam	blue	black	pale	Outstanding	200
19	Monaghan, Wm.,	51	Crossrenagh	blue	black	ruddy	Outstanding	194
20	Gaughan, John, .	33	Gladree	blue	dark	pale	Flat, lobes attached	196
21	Reilly, Peter, .	35	Duvillaun (?)	blue	brown	ruddy	Flat, lobes absent	200
22	Barrett, Michael,	44	Drumreagh	light-grey	black	ruddy	Outstanding, lobes absent	196
23	Barrett, William,	30	Mullaghroe	blue	brown	ruddy	Outstanding, lobes attached	200
24	Henry, Phelim,	40	Name of locality not decipherable	blue	brown	ruddy	Outstanding, lobes attached	199
25	Coyle, Michael, .	18	Belmullet	blue	dark	pale	Outstanding	191
26	M'Cormac, Thos.,	21	Aughaglassheen, Belmullet	dark-grey	dark	dark	Outstanding, lobes attached	195
27	Doocy, Patrick, .	19	Porturlin	blue	dark	pale	Outstanding	190
28	Flannery, Thos.,	60	Srahataggle	light-grey	dark	pale	Outstanding	194
29	Gannon, Richard,	26	Carrowboy (?)	light-grey	black	ruddy	Outstanding	194
30	Dogherty, Wm.,	21	Portacloy	green	red	ruddy	Outstanding, lobes attached	196
31	Naughton, Michl.	40	Portacloy	blue	dark	ruddy	Flat, lobes absent	190

Length.	Breadth.	Internal Bi-nocular bdth.	Cranial Height.	Nasial.	Alveolar.	Standing.	Sitting.	Span.	Hand.	Forearm.	Remarks.
54	36	32	130	101	99	1775	935	1880	195	261	" King" of Inishkea.
53	34	30	126	103	98	1700	912	1730	185	251	Brother of No. 1.
60	38	36	130	96	94	1780	960	1781	200	272	Mother from N. Inishkea.
54	34	36	125	97	95	1696	895	1652	185	254	Brother of No. 3; beard fair.
60	36	34	127	96	98	1757	908	1830	200	275	Front teeth even.
60	34	32	126	100	101	1780	888	1865	206	275	Beard brown.
50	34	32	125	88	88	1691	902	1720	180	250	Nose sinuous.
52	34	33	129	95	88	1766	955	1765	187	270	Brother of No. 7; nose sinuous.
56	32	31	126	93	93	1710	900	1763	190	250	—
48	33	29	130	94	96	1640	852	1612	173	260	Brother of No. 9: beard fair.
58	36	26	129	90	88	1708	914	1730	181	246	—
51	43	32	130	95	95	1664	858	1810	200	240	*Nez rétroussé.*
66	30	29	120	95	91	1660	855	1780	197	261	—
57	30	27	126	88	89	1757	925	1777	210	272	People originally from Ballycroy.
59	34	33	128	95	94	1762	925	—	200	266	People originally from Donegal, 200 years ago.
52	38	31	127	100	106	1708	928	1795	199	256	—
55	36	35	125	97	107	1732	885	1816	195	292	—
55	33	37	135	97	103	1766	930	1814	203	276	—
55	32	29	126	95	100	1770	917	1875	198	279	—
57	32	29	132	95	100	1820	923	1865	212	270	Father's people from Ballycroy.
54	30	29	125	96	104	1723	921	1793	200	288	—
49	36	36	128	96	95	1716	905	1870	204	271	Beard dark-brown.
51	38	30	133	97	99	1674	888	1793	191	277	Descended from the Clan Barretts, of " the Proud House of Barret" in the Mullet.
55	29	31	129	97	95	1687	952	1775	198	286	People originally from Donegal.
54	33	30	128	95	97	1743	887	1820	200	264	—
51	33	31	133	93	98	1685	905	1723	188	248	—
57	34	28	125	95	94	1628	880	1778	189	257	Believes grand-father to have been French.
55	30	29	127	92	93	1701	880	1712	193	267	—
53	30	30	130	91	89	1820	942	1850	198	271	—
53	31	29	129	89	93	1767	945	1843	207	270	Ancestors from Ulster.
56	32	29	125	95	97	1707	920	1775	195	261	—

No.	Name.	Age.	Locality.	Eye Colour.	Hair Colour.	Skin.	Ears.	CEPH Length.
32	Magrath, Patk., .	44	Portacloy	blue	dark	pale	Flat	178
33	Bourne, William,	33	Portacloy	light-grey	brown	ruddy	Flat	199
34	Bourke, John, .	33	Portacloy	blue	dark	ruddy	Flat, lobes attached	200
35	Toole, Thomas, .	33	Portacloy	blue	dark	ruddy	Outstanding	189
36	Hogan, John, .	40	Portacloy	blue	dark	ruddy	Flat, lobes attached	194
37	Bourke, Domk., .	21	Portacloy	blue	dark	ruddy	Flat	203
38	Hevernan, Philip,	50	Aughleam, Mullet	light-grey	dark	ruddy	Outstanding	200
39	Reilly, James, .	35	Drum, Mullet	light-grey	brown	pale	Outstanding	198
40	Kane, Richard, .	—	Fallmore, Mullet	green	brown	—	Outstanding	211
41	————	—	Mullet	blue	brown	pale & freck-led-	Outstanding	186
42	M'Loughlin, Th.,	25	Blacksod, Mullet	blue	brown	pale	Flat	197
43	Meenaghan, Th.,	18	Blacksod, Mullet	light-grey	brown	ruddy	Outstanding, lobes attached	196
44	Dixon, ——,	50	Tip., Mullet	blue	dark	dark	Attached lobules	196
45	Cafferky, Hugh, .	—	Tip., Mullet	blue	brown	ruddy	Attached lobules	198
46	Coyle, Francis, .	47	Tip., Mullet	blue	dark	ruddy	Flat	204
47	Padden, Domk., .	22	Tip., Mullet	blue	brown	pale	Outstanding, lobes absent	196
48	Padden, John, .	18	Tip., Mullet	blue	dark	pale, freck-led	Flat, lobes absent	194
49	Dixon, James, .	28	Tip., Mullet	blue	brown	pale	Flat, lobes absent	200
50	Lavelle, Anthony,	24	Tip., Mullet	green	black	ruddy	Flat, lobes absent	206
51	Meenaghan, Ml.,	—	Inishkea, S.	green	dark	ruddy	Flat, lobes at-tached	196
52	M'Ginty, Owen, .	35	Inishkea, S.	blue	black-brown	ruddy	Outstanding, lobes attached	208
53	Monaghan, Ml., .	59	Inishkea, S.	light-brown	black	dark	Outstanding	192
54	Keane, Patrick, .	19	Inishkea, S.	blue	fair	ruddy, freck-led	Outstanding	195
55	O'Donnell, John,	24	Inishkea, S.	blue	fair	ruddy, freck-led	Outstanding, lobes attached	204
56	Dixon, Patrick, .	33	Aghadoon, Mullet	blue	brown	ruddy	Flat	204
57	Carey, Martin, .	26	Aghadoon, Mullet	dark-grey	black	ruddy	Outstanding, lobes absent	194
58	Lavelle, Patrick,	30	Aghadoon, Mullet	blue	dark	ruddy	Flat	202
59	Dixon, Patrick, .	30	Aghadoon, Mullet	green	black	pale	Flat	208
60	Burke, John, .	23	Belmullet	blue	brown	ruddy	Flat, lobes attached	194
61	Joyce, Patrick, .	18	Buncrena, Mullet	blue	fair	ruddy	Outstanding	191
62	Padden, Michael,	22	Knockna-shambo, Mullet	blue	brown	dark	Flat, lobes attached	195

Face length.	Upper Face length.	Breadth.	Bigonial Breadth.	Length.	Breadth.	Internal Binocular bdth.	Cranial Height.	Nasal.	Alveolar.	Standing.	Sitting.	Span.	Hand.	Forearm.	Remarks.
114	69	140	112	53	33	27	122	95	91	1726	923	1800	204	260	—
132	78	142	113	58	31	31	129	101	103	1782	970	1930	213	277	Name is an Anglicized form of O'Conboirne.
114	68	146	110	49	34	31	133	98	108	1711	946	1870	200	274	—
120	72	132	111	49	30	28	125	91	90	1709	932	1750	181	257	—
133	77	139	102	54	36	35	125	97	105	1730	903	1838	188	286	Father's people from Co. Clare, 50 years ago.
121	75	140	121	52	32	31	133	96	89	1758	952	1960	198	273	—
134	77	143	118	56	40	32	127	101	109	1764	950	1860	196	270	—
123	76	139	108	56	34	32	131	92	95	1776	945	1920	209	266	—
132	75	150	110	57	38	32	145	97	95	1805	973	1853	192	263	—
125	74	148	104	54	33	28	133	95	86	1730	927	1830	195	264	Did not give name; mother's name Lynsky.
120	73	145	120	53	36	33	127	100	100	1730	903	1718	193	263	Beard fair.
122	72	147	114	49	34	34	132	95	99	1674	198	1727	188	252	—
125	76	141	116	48	35	30	127	96	98	1640	905	1678	192	256	—
125	76	138	110	57	35	30	130	101	101	1744	920	1822	197	273	Nose slightly aquiline.
126	72	143	108	55	40	35	132	99	105	1721	921	1810	204	250	—
124	75	138	112	52	32	37	126	104	103	1683	885	1826	191	272	Nose sinuous.
122	71	141	110	55	33	34	133	103	99	1752	925	1866	200	275	—
126	76	148	118	53	35	33	132	101	102	1746	950	1850	193	264	—
131	71	154	124	50	33	35	138	105	109	1788	945	1870	198	269	Extremely muscular.
119	73	138	112	49	37	32	125	92	92	1690	877	1785	197	244	Nose sinuous.
133	77	146	118	58	36	27	140	91	90	1725	910	1805	200	260	—
132	74	138	108	53	35	20	126	93	93	1650	840	1765	202	269	—
110	63	142	111	45	33	36	134	93	95	1697	860	1775	203	265	—
123	67	146	118	48	37	32	133	95	90	1692	926	1800	193	263	Father's people from Co. Galway.
131	72	144	126	50	37	31	131	98	98	1810	963	1991	205	298	—
117	73	144	114	53	33	33	133	102	99	1675	885	1816	195	270	Folds of pinna obliterated.
117	67	143	120	48	35	33	126	99	100	1642	865	1700	182	253	—
134	77	140	115	52	34	31	137	102	102	1707	905	1785	190	264	—
130	74	140	118	56	31	34	132	94	96	1794	920	1875	195	286	—
124	77	140	112	57	33	28	134	96	96	1697	903	1720	191	270	—
129	75	145	118	53	39	30	130	100	100	1703	934	1780	193	271	—

(E.) *Analysis of the Statistical Tables* :—

The variations in type in the inhabitants of the different parts of the district are shown by the following Table, which appears to corroborate the belief entertained by the people that the men of North Inishkea are taller than those of the South Island or of the Mullet. They also show the greater proportion of light hair in the islanders :

	Mullet.	North Inishkea.	South Inishkea.	Portacloy.
Number measured,	35	8	7	12
Cephalic Index,	79·5	78·4	80·1	80·0
Stature,	1704 (5 ft. 7 in.)	1727 (5 ft. 8 in.)	1705 (5 ft. 7 in.)	1727 (5 ft. 8 in.)
Proportion to stature—Span,	104·55	102·45	103·58	105·65
,, ,, Hand,	11·34	11·04	11·41	11·41
,, ,, Forearm,	15·47	15·60	15·32	15·57
Nigrescence Index,[1]	62·30	10·5		77·52

Though the people in all sections of the district are seen to be mesaticephalic (if two units be subtracted to reduce the index to cranial standard), yet in two, South Inishkea and Portacloy, there is an approach to the brachycephalic form. None of the men measured in either place are dolichocephalic, and in most cases the cephalic proportion inclines towards the higher index rather than to the lower.

It would appear also that the North Inishkea men are shorter-limbed than any of their neighbours, as out of the four cases met with in which the span (*grande envergue*) was less than the height, three were from this island.

3. *Vital Statistics* (*General and Economic*) :—

(A.) *Population.* — Erris is not now very thickly peopled, the general decrease affecting the population of Ireland during the last fifty years having especially affected this district.

The census returns show a constant and steady decline since 1851, the slight increases which have from time to time occurred in some

---

[1] Not taken from number measured but from nigrescence cards.

townlands having only been temporary. That this loss is entirely due to emigration is proved by the returns of births and deaths in the registration district of Binghamstown for the decennial period 1884–1893 in which space of time the births numbered 1260, and the deaths 707, an excess of 553, or 22·7 per cent. The following Table, which refers only to the parish of Kilmore, shows the population of the district at each census since 1851, with the number of inhabited houses, average number of inhabitants per house, and of acres per head.[1]

Census.	Population.	Houses.	Inhabitants. per house.	Acres per head.
1851	7379	1106	6·67	3·99
1861	6452	1243	5·19	4·57
1871	5552	1054	5·27	5·31
1881	5327	911	5·85	5·53
1891	4111	694	5·92	7·17

The density of population is thus seen to be about 89 per square mile, but varies with locality, being greatest on S. Inishkea, where it is about 304.

The town of Belmullet, which is not included in the table given above, has fluctuated much since its foundation in 1825. In 1831 its population was 585, and it continued to increase until after 1851, when it had attained its maximum of 935; from that time forth it declined. In 1861 its inhabitants numbered 907; in 1871, 849; in 1881 there was a slight increase, 852; and at the last census, in 1891, the population had fallen to 652.

It was difficult to lay down any exact boundaries to what, for the purposes of this report, is termed the Portacloy district; but the three townlands—Srahataggle, Portacloy, and Curraunboy, from which most of those measured at Portacloy came, have been taken to represent it; in these the population has not undergone the same change as that of Kilmore, the population having risen since 1851, from 248, inhabiting 46 houses, to 299 in 53 houses.

---

[1] In 1831 the population of Kilmore Erris was 9287.

The distribution of population, inhabited houses, and outbuildings
was as follows in 1891 :—

Locality.	Area.	POPULATION.			Houses.	Outbuild-ings and Farm-steadings.
		Persons.	Males.	Females.		
	A. R. P.					
The Mullet, .	23,333 1 27	3757	1893	1864	600	532
N. Inishkea, .	464 1 32	126	60	66	21	4
S. Inishkea, .	344 3 19	180	92	88	32	33
23 Islets, . .	350 0 17	48	22	26	10	27
Portacloy, .	7845 1 1	299	148	151	54	29
Totals, . . .	32,338 0 16	4410	2215	2195	717	625

(B.) *Acreage and Rental.*—The total area of the district is that of
Kilmore, being 29,492 acres, and the three townlands forming the
Portacloy district, 7,845 acres.

The total valuation of Kilmore is £4,055 18s., and of Portacloy
£163 7s.

There is very little commonage in the Mullet, but about Portacloy
there is a good deal.

The holdings are not large, averaging about 4½ or 5 acres at a
rental of about £3 10s. in the Mullet, and about £2 10s. in "the
mountains." There is considerable variation, however, as there are
some farms of good size, but the majority are small.

In 1891 there were, in Kilmore, 210 holdings of between £4 and
£10 valuation, 305 of £2 and under £4, and no less than 252 at,
or under, £2 valuation.

The land is mostly held now at judicial rentals (the people having
early taken advantage of the Land Act of 1881), but sixty years ago
the greater part of the land was held in common, and the mode of
tenure is thus described by Knight :—" In the whole of the peninsula
there are few farms divided . . . the usual system being commonage
both in tillage and pasture. In tillage, lots are cast every third
year for the number of ridges each person is entitled to after the
usual rotation is over. Potatoes the first year, then burley or oats,
after which new lots must be cast for new potato ground. The
holdings are by sums or collops, which originally meant the number

of heads of cattle the farm could rear by *pasture*; but as some tillage became afterwards necessary, they divided the crop-ground into collops also, as well as the pasture, and each farm then had its number of tillage collops and of grazing collops. The tillage collop is supposed to be capable of supporting one family by its produce. In many instances poor families have no pasture to correspond with their tillage collop, and even of this they may have only a half or quarter, called a *geerla*. . . . The prices of these collops vary according to the quality of the farm; the average is about one guinea. The pasture collop is the grass of a horse, or a cow, or two year old heifers, or six or eight sheep. It is evident from this system, that although a man may expend a good deal of labour in digging and manuring his ridge, it is only a chance whether he will enjoy the labour so expended the third year, and hence that he is careless of future benefits, and that, of course, the land will be but imperfectly cultivated. . . . There is a headman or *king* appointed in every village, who is deputed to cast the lots every third year, and to arrange with the community what work is to be done during the year in fencing, &c. . . . The king takes care generally to have the rent collected, applots the proportion of taxes with the other elders of the village, for all is done in a patriarchal way, *coram populo.*"

The following table, extracted from Mr. Knight's valuable little book on Erris (p. 58), is given here as illustrating the condition of people sixty years ago.

KNIGHT'S POPULATION TABLE.

Population, &c.		Remarks.
Families,	1723	
Males,	4290 ⎫ 8662	By public census, in the year 1831, 9287; but I believe this to be more correct. The whole Barony, in 1821, was 17,879; in 1831, 22,824.
Females,	4372 ⎭	
Rental,	£4300	Or about 50s. to each family.
Sums or collops,	4469	Green acres as before 6100; collops different in size and quality, more than 2½ to each family.
Amount of Tithes,	£258	There is no composition, the old mode followed in collecting. There is now (1834) a composition for £300.
Boats (sail),	5	These six items show the little attention paid to the fishing, one boat of *every* kind in thirteen families, and one net in every seven. Three or four families frequently join in a boat, and two or three in a herring net, or set of nets.
Boats (row),	88	
Curraghs,	38	
Nets,	256	
Lines,	131	
Spillets,	8	

Population, &c.		Remarks.
Horses, . . . 587 ⎱ 943		Or only one beast of burden nearly, to every two families. Major Bingham and a few others have some good horses. The general breed is small, but hardy.
Asses, . . . 356 ⎰		
Cows, ... 1967		This is more than one to each family.
Sheep, . . . 2348		
Pigs, . . . 919		
Ploughs,		At Major Bingham's, Rev. Mr. Dawson's, and Rev. Mr. Lyons's.
Carts, .		Same.
Feather beds, . . 624		Or nearly one to every third family. The substitute—straw, rushes, or bent.
Blankets, . . . 1838		
Men without shoes, . 734		
Men, women, and children, 3156		Wanting clothes, or nearly one-third of the whole population.
Buying provisions, . . 751		In a year of great plenty, but after two of great scarcity.
Sick, ... 454		
Died (1831), . . . 236		
Carriages (four-wheeled), 2		
Carriages (two-wheeled), 8		

(c.) *Language and Illiteracy—Language.*—1 regret to be unable to give here the proportion of people speaking Irish alone, and Irish and English, as the census authorities make the return by baronies only. The great majority of the people are bi-lingual, speaking both Irish and English, employing Irish mainly when speaking among themselves, but there is some small proportion, especially among the older people, who speak no English. The inhabitants of Inishkea do not usually speak anything but Irish on their own islands, though having a fair knowledge of English; but many of the women on these islands have no knowledge of the last-named language. About Portacloy there are many who " have no English."

Illiteracy.—The return for this is given by parishes. In Kilmore, in 1891, there were 3590 persons of five years old and upwards; of these 2135 or 59·5 per. cent. were illiterate.

	Persons.	Male.	Female.
Number above 5 years,	3590	1811	1779
Illiterate, . . .	2135	978	1157
Percentage, . .	59·5	54·0	65·0

(D.) *Health.*—It was found to be a difficult matter to obtain reliable information on this point, but there seems to be, on the whole, but little serious disease, and the people appear to be strong and healthy. The affections suffered from are mainly due to the nature of their food and occupations, and the unwholesome state of their dwellings.

Consanguineous Marriages.—The intermarriage of relations seems to be very common, not only on the islands, but also on the mainland, where it is most common in small fishing hamlets difficult of access, such as Fallmore, Tip, and Portacloy. While visiting Inishkea inquiries were made as to these unions, and several of the inhabitants assured me that intermarriage between the people of the North and South Islands was not common, it being a far more usual thing for the islanders to marry people from the opposite shore of the Mullet; thus, the South Island people seem to intermarry a good deal with the inhabitants of Fallmore, a very primitive village at the extreme end of the peninsula, which has only being provided with a road, such as it is, since 1881. On both islands, however, the majority of the marriages seem to take place between members of the community.

It does not seem as if it were usual for first cousins to marry, but matches between relatives of all degrees farther out seem to be of very common occurrence.

Through the kindness of the Rev. H. Hewson, P.P. of Belmullet, I am enabled to give actual figures, as he has kept the record of dispensations for these marriages since 1875; from that date until August, 1894, there were in the Parish of Kilmore, which contains about 700 families, altogether 276 marriages, and of these 61 or 22·1 per cent. obtained dispensations, as the parties were relatives. In the Parish of Belmullet, number of families 460, there were in the same period 247 with 26 consanguineous (or 10·5 per cent.) and Kilcommon, with about 620 families, had 276 marriages, for 72 of which, or 26·1 per cent., dispensations were granted. The average in the whole three parishes was thus 19·5 per cent. To these may be added some 10 or 12 more cases of marriages of first cousins dispensed by the bishop of the diocese. There does not seem to be any marked result from this long continued close intermarriage, except the very marked local types observable in the more isolated places, which seem to have been fixed or preserved by this cause. This is especially the case in the islands whose inhabitants, while bearing a general resemblance to each other, differ much in appearance from their neighbours of the mainland.

It has been stated by one or two casual visitors that the natives of Inishkea were dwarfed and very degenerate, but this idea seems to have arisen from the islands having been visited at a time when most of the able-bodied men were away at the lobster-fishery, and only the immature, the old, and the ailing were at home. No man of less than 1640 m.m. (5 ft. 4½ in.) was met with on either island, and the men appear to be robust and athletic, while the women are, on the whole, good looking.

The people themselves do not seem to ascribe any ill effects to the close intermarriage. It is doubtful if these unions are proportionally more frequent in Inishkea than on the mainland.

Diseases.—The following account is believed to be correct, though, as before stated, there was much difficulty in obtaining accurate information on this subject. Actual figures are given wherever they could be obtained.

The principal diseases may be classed as follows :—

Insanity.—A considerable number of cases occur in Erris, mainly in the mountainous districts, comparatively few in the Mullet, and, all informants agreed in stating, that there have been none for many years from either north or south Inishkea.

The prevalence of insanity in the mountainous regions may probably be partly due to illicit distillation, and the influences of worse food and inferior dwellings compared to those of the people of the coast.

Idiocy and Imbecility.—Repeated inquiries failed to find more than two imbeciles, one on south Inishkea, and the other in Belmullet. Two members of the family in the south Inishkea case are lame ; no history could be obtained relative to the parents.

Epilepsy is not very common, but several cases (number not ascertained) are known ; none of these are in the islands.

Deaf-mutism.—There is one case of deaf-mutism in Belmullet. Parents were said not to be related. No cases in the peninsula or on the islands.

Blindness, except among the aged, is not common. A congenitally blind boy was drowned in the year 1893, trying to cross in a curragh from one of the islands to the mainland with a cargo of poteen.

Malformations seem to be rare, two cases of hare lip were the only ones seen, and the inquiry failed to find any more except the two cases of lameness mentioned above.

Fevers.—Enteric and typhus are both common, cases of the latter being of frequent occurence. Measles and scarlet fever are not very often met with.

" *Constitutional* " *diseases.*—Phthisis and struma are stated to be comparatively rare.

Malignant disease is very common in the Mullet, especially in the electoral district of Binghamstown South, which includes all the southern part of the peninsula. The majority of these cases are said to fall into the hands of "cancer curers," who use arsenic paste.

Rheumatism is one of the most prevalent troubles, especially in the elderly and old.

" Gravel " is a common complaint all over the district, and a good many deaths from this cause are registered.

Dietetic diseases.—Digestive troubles are very common everywhere, but more especially in the inland parts where the dietary is less varied ; " boxty," or potato-bread and the abuse of strong tea seem to be very largely responsible.

Along the coast, ento-parasites, due to the large proportion of fish in the dietary, are of very frequent occurence.

Respiratory diseases.—Bronchitis is very prevalent in the winter and spring, and spasmodic asthma is stated to be not an uncommon affection.

Local affections are few and not very serious. Conjunctivitis is common, and much aggravated by the peat-smoke of the houses.

As regards dental troubles, the people are by no means free from these, though as a rule the teeth are even and white, and remain sound until late in life.

" Female " troubles seem to be very common.

Venereal diseases are practically non-existant.

Skin.—Skin diseases are very prevalent. Among these the most common are—tinea tonsurans, eczema, sea boils, and scabies.

Accidental injuries.—Owing to the mode of life of the people and their environment, accidents frequently happen, especially fractures and contusions from falls, bites and other injuries from domestic animals, and burns.

4. *Psychology.*—The difficulties of treating this part of the subject justly are, in the case of a stranger, very great, as his acquaintance with the people cannot be of sufficiently long standing to allow of the knowledge of more than the superficial part of their character, while, in the case of a resident, personal likes and antipathies, and local quarrels or friendships, largely influence his opinions.

The following description, though to some extent derived from personal observation, is for the most part obtained from several local sources, my informants being those who are brought into close contact with the everyday life of the people. So far as it goes it is believed to be accurate. No attempt has been made to do otherwise than describe the actual state of the case, and while the faults of the people are not extenuated, yet any circumstances which may explain these are given as far as possible, and their good qualities are believed to be stated without exaggeration.

To the casual visitor the people, on acquaintance, are decidedly attractive ; in the outlying parts of the district, it is true, they are at first rather suspicious of strangers, but after a short time are very obliging and communicative, ready to show anything of interest in their neighbourhood, and hospitable to the best of their power. The natives of both the islands at Inishkea, are very hospitable and kindly to strangers, of whom they are, however, rather distrustful, a visitor being welcomed into their houses, and entertained with the best they can give. With each other they seem in all parts of the district to be much given to chaff and joking of a more or less practical nature, and their sense of the ridiculous seems to be rather keen. In times of trouble or distress they are very kind, generous with what they have, and helpful to one another.

They are fond of music, dancing, and bright colours, and more than one song-maker in their own tongue, the Irish, has been a native of this district ; amongst these was the celebrated Dick Barrett, several of whose productions have been collected and published. In common with most of the people of our rural districts, there do not seem to be many traces of artistic taste, and a native art is conspicious by its absence. One or two instances of attempted decoration were observed in Inishkea, none on the mainland.

On the whole, though cases of dishonesty and sharp practice in bargaining occur, they are honest in their dealings with one another. As is often the case in remote districts, the people of one locality are sometimes on strained relations with those of another ; thus there exists a certain amount of jealousy and distrust between the natives of the two Inishkeas, while the people of the mainland do not readily amalgamate with those of either island.

As regards intelligence, they are extremely sharp and shrewd, and seem rather fond of argumentation. There is but little crime, with the exception of illicit distillation and drunkenness, but the people are very litigious, going to law with each other about slight trespasses and similar matters. This tendency is not by any means of recent origin, but has been remarked on by several writers. Maxwell mentions that at one time the people of Inishkea were much noted for it, and that the fate of the two men, who some time in the last century ruined themselves in a lawsuit about a sheep, became proverbial, and litigants were warned to remember the fate of "Malley and Malone." C. O.[1] also refers to this peculiarity, which nowadays seems to be more characteristic of the mainland people than the islanders.

In the course of the cases arising from this tendency, many curious examples of ingenious cross-swearing occur. Intoxication is rather prevalent on fair days and holidays, and at weddings and other festive occasions, but at ordinary times there is not much of it among the country people. They appear to be conscientious in their religious observances, and depend much on the guidance and advice of their clergy.

As will be judged from the extent and variety of their folk-lore, they have a great love for the supernatural and mystical.

As regards morals, though illegitimacy is by no means unknown, yet, when the size of the population is taken into account, it is so rare as to be very creditable to the moral tone of the people.[2]

A stand-up fight rarely occurs when men quarrel, there may be one or two blows struck, or stone-throwing may be indulged in, but disputes do not usually get beyond cursing and vituperation.

As parents they are affectionate, but careless and unequal in their treatment of their children, at one time over indulging them, and at another punishing severely for a slight fault.

With regard to industry, but little can be said in their favour, though energetic by starts, during which they are capable of a great deal of work, accounts agree in stating that they dislike steady occupation, and are indolent. It should be remembered, however, that there has hitherto been but little inducement to them to cultivate steady industry. The women seem always to have plenty of work on hand, and to do it.

In this district, as in many others, the people are not very careful in their re-payment of debts, and shopkeepers do not now give credit to the same extent as formerly. As to rent and cess, to the payment of these, too, a strong aversion is often manifested.

Many of their habits are not over cleanly, though this is largely due to the wretched nature of their houses, and a strict regard for truth is not a prominent part of their character.

---

[1] "Sketches in Erris and Tyrawley."

[2] The total number of cases which occurred between the years 1884 and 1893 was 18.

5. *Folk Names.*—The following list of surnames was obtained, comprising all those of the district, with the exception of a few new comers, and the names of the inhabitants of the town of Belmullet :—

Surname.	Number of Families.	Surname.	Number of Families.
Barrett,	27	Garrett,	1
Bingham,	3	Gavan,	2
Boland,	1	Gaughan,	23
Boylan,	2	Gaynard,	4
Brotherick,	3	Geoghan,	2
Burnes,	3	Geraghty,	15
Burke,	2	Gibbon,	1
Carden,	1[1]	Gilbert,	1
Carey,	12	Gilboy,	1
Cattigan,	2	Ginnelly.	8
Caufield,	1	Ginnings,	1
Cawley,	13	Ginty,	1
Connell,	2	Goonan,	1
Connolly,	1	Gonigal,	1
Connor,	2	Hannely,	1
Conroy,	3	Haveron,	7
Conway,	3	Henry,	1
Costello,	1	Henaghan,	4
Cosgrove,	1	Heaveran,	3
Coyle,	5	Hogan,	1
Crnine,	7	Hopkins,	1
Cuff,	1	Horkin,	4
Curduff,	4	Howard.	3
Curley,	1	Hughes,	1
Davitt,	3	Joyce,	7
Deane,	8	Keane,	5
Dent,	1	Kelly,	5
Devanny,	1	Keeraghan,	1
Diamond,	2	Kearney,	1
Dinnery,	2	Kennedy,	6
Diver,	2	Kilker,	3
Dixon,	16	Kilkoyne.	1
Dogherty,	1	King,	1
Doogan,	2	Lally,	9
Dunleavy,	4	Langan,	1
Earley,	6	Lavelle,	31
Egan,	2	Lenaghan	1
Follan,	1	Loftus,	1
Friel,	1	Lynch,	1
Gallagher,	8	Lynskey,	2
Gammell,	1	Lyons,	1
Gannon,	3	Malowney.	1
Garvan,	1	M'Andrew,	8

[1] Not native.

LIST OF SURNAMES—*continued.*

Surname.	Number of Families.	Surname.	Number of Families.
M'Cormack,	1	Neely,	1
M'Dermott,	1	O'Boy,	1
M'Donnell,	6	O'Donnell,	4
M'Loughlin,	1	O'Mallen,	1
M'Ginty,	4	O'Malley,	2
M'Grath,	5	Padden,	16
M'Guinness,	2	Palmer,	1
M'Hale,	4	Philbin,	3
M'Intyre,	3	Quigley,	1
M'Mannam,	2	Reilly,	27
M'Namara,	1	Richards,	1
M'Neely,	1	Ruane,	5
M'Nulty,	3	Ruddy,	7
Meenaghan,	14	Scanlon,	2
Monaghan,	20	Tighe,	10
Monnelly,	4	Togher,	12
Monghan,	4	Tollet,	1
Moran,	1	Toole,	2
Mullaney,	1	Walker,	2
Murphy,	9	Walshe,	10
Murray,	4	Ward,	1
Nallon,	2	Williams,	4
Neary,	1	Wilson,	4

While the original localities of some of these names are easily traced, those of others are very obscure, and this for several reasons: one of these is the anglicising of old Irish surnames, often into forms bearing little or no resemblance to the original; which here, as in other parts of the country, has taken place to a very great extent: a second is the hibernicising of the names and branches of Welsh and Anglo-Norman families, *e.g.* M'Andrew, which has been adopted by a branch of the Barretts: a third difficulty is the use by many of the people of double surnames, one employed when speaking Irish, the other in speaking English; thus, Togher is anglicised Swift.

The following names are traceable, either by tradition, or by historical evidence.

(A.) The ancient surnames of the territory (Hy Fiachrach), in which this district was included, still persist to a large extent, though in altered forms; and all the principal of these now extant, as far as could be ascertained, are given below in both the ancient and the modern forms.

Modern Form.	Ancient Name.
Boland, . . .	O'Beollain.
Burnes, . . .	Mac Conboirne.
Conroy, . . .	O'Mailchonairi.
Connolly, . .	Mac Conghaile.
Crain or Crean, .	O'Criadhchen.
Doogan = Egan, .	Mac Egan.
Earley, . . .	O'Mailfomhair.
Friel, . . .	O'Farghil (from Ulster originally).
Gannon, . . .	Mag Fhionnain.
Gaughan, . . .	O'Gaibhtheachain.
Heaveran & Haveron,	O'Fuathmharain.
Henaghan, . .	O'h-Eidhneachan.
Hughes, . . .	O'h-Aodha.
Kean, or Kane, .	O'Cathan, or O'Caithneadh.
Kearney, . . .	O'Cearnaigh.
Lavelle, . . .	O'Maolfabhaill.
Loftus, . . .	O'Lachtna.
Lyons, . . .	O'Liathain (?).
Mac Dermott, . .	————
Mac Hale, . .	Mac Cele.
Mac Grath, . .	O'Moran.
Meenaghan, . .	O'Muinhneachain.
Moran, . . .	O'Moran.
Monghan, . .	Mochain (originally from Roscommon) (?).
Murphy, . . .	O'Murchada.
Murray, . . .	O'Muireadhaigh.
Ruane, . . .	O'Ruaidhin.
Ruddy, . . .	Brodaibh.
Scanlon, . . .	Scanlain.

Although these are the only names which I have been able to trace, (chiefly from O'Donovan), yet there can be no doubt that many other surnames of the region are quite as long established, though the families bearing them may not have been of sufficient historical importance to have received record.

(B.) The next in order of antiquity are Welsh or Anglo-Norman families, who, for so long, held the reins of power in this part of

Ireland. Barrett, Burke, Carey, Joyce, M'Andrew, Walsh, and probably Williams (if it be, as is alleged, a form of Mac William or
Mac Quillin).

(c.) The immigrants from Ulster come next, amongst whose
descendants are said to be the O'Donnells, Connells, Doghertys,
Gallaghers, Geraghtys, Reillys (from Cavan), and perhaps M'Loughlins.

(D.) The Mac Cormicks came into the district in the reign of
James I.

(E.) Last come names of English origin, the most ancient of which
seems to be Bingham, dating from the reign of Elizabeth. Tollet, and
probably Dixon, are names of descendants of the Shane settlers. The
other English names are of shorter standing, and some of them may
really be anglicised local surnames.

The names of the English settlers signed to the petition to Sir
Henry Bingham, sometime in the reign of Queen Anne, are Higgin-
botham, Maxwell, Dennistoun, Linney, Langford, Tollett, Houston,
Parker, Gamble, Calwell, and Low; of these, Tollett is the only one
now found in the parish, if Gammell be not a corrupted form of
Gamble.[1]

IV.—Sociology.

1. *Occupations.*—Excluding the inhabitants of the little town of
Belmullet, in which most of the tradesmen reside, the people are, as
a rule, either fishermen or farmers, or they combine both occupations.
There are a few large holders and proprietors, but the majority of the
farms are of small size. These holdings are but poorly fenced, a
frequent cause of dispute. Fences are usually earthen or turf, but on
the islands dry stone walls, such as are seen in Aran, are common.
The principal crops are barley, oats, rye, and potatoes. All the farming
is rude and primitive. Spade labour is practically universal, the
spades being of modern form, as the old " gowel "[2] or " gowel-gob," a
two-bladed or forked wooden spade formerly used here, has long been
extinct.

In 1834 there were only 3 ploughs and the same number of carts
in use in the Mullet : now (1895) the number of ploughs is 30, and of
carts 63.

---

[1] Though these settlers are spoken of as English by the various writers who
have mentioned the colony, yet the majority of these surnames appear to be Scotch.
[2] A specimen of this curious agricultural implement is figured in the Catalogue
of Antiquities of the Royal Irish Academy.

The manures used are mainly sea-weed and farmyard manure. In the mountains the practice of burning the land is common.

The pasture is fairly good, but the cattle and sheep are inferior, though efforts are now being made to improve the breeds.

An average family has a couple of pigs, a cow or two and some sheep, a large number of fowl, geese and ducks, and a donkey or horse.

The fuel used is turf obtained from the bogs, which are extensive, except in the southern part of the Mullet ; and the islands which have now no turf of their own import from Achill or Ballycroy.

A very considerable quantity of kelp is made, on which, in the Mullet, a royalty is charged by the landlord. About Portacloy there is no royalty paid.

Fishing employs many of the men, though until lately the fish taken was merely for home use. The kinds usually caught are turbot, mackerel, ling, cod, and herrings; all of these, except the turbot, are now cured at the fishing stations established at several parts of the coast by the government. For home consumption, much is eaten fresh, but a good deal of it is roughly salted for winter use.

Lobsters are mostly taken by the men of Inishkea, and by a couple of boats at Portacloy. The Inishkea men, while at this fishing, mostly live in very primitive huts on Inisglora, where they stay away from their families for six weeks or two months at a time. The lobsters are sold in Belmullet for about five shillings per dozen, and are sent by car to Ballina and thence to England. The lobster pots are mostly of home manufacture.

The fishery stations mentioned above now afford employment to many who formerly had no means of disposing of their surplus time and fish.

Large quantities of eggs are exported from this district, Belmullet being the largest egg exporting centre in Ireland. They are brought into the town by the country people and sold to dealers, who, when they have collected a sufficient quantity, send them on to Ballina, whence they are sent to England. Butter is also exported in the summer and autumn.

Illicit distilling is carried on to some extent in this district, though not at all so prevalent as formerly. The stills are made in the people's homes by travelling tinkers who live with the family until the job is finished.

A good deal of homespun is made, but the dyes are not obtained from plants growing in the district as formerly, but are imported. There are several weavers in the district, and the clothes are made up by a local tailor. One unusual occupation, that of cloth miller or presser is carried on by a man in Belmullet, who uses a rather primitive press of his own construction.

There is very little regular employment for labourers, except that given by a few of the resident gentry and some of the people of Belmullet. Labourers receive 1s. 6d. a day, or a 1s. and their food; if at harvest time, threshing or employed at cutting turf, slightly more, about 2s. a day.

Little or no work is done by the majority of the men during the winter months, except to gather a little drift weed along the coast.

The women attend to the ordinary duties of the house, assist at field work and at bringing home turf; they gather and dry carrageen moss (*sphaerococcus crispus*) which they sell at the rate of 2s. a stone (unbleached); they also card and spin the wool. Old women often get employment going from house to house oiling, carding, and spinning the wool for the household; for this work they receive 2s. a week and their keep.

2. *Family Life and Customs.*—The general characters of family life are much the same as those of the people of Inishbofin.

The children, who are usually numerous, are sent to school, if at all, at about five years of age; they show plenty of aptness at acquiring knowledge, but as their attendance is very irregular, through their being wanted at home to help their parents, their progress is much impeded. When they reach the age of fourteen or fifteen years they leave school and enter into the regular work of the household until they have attained means either to marry and settle down or to emigrate.

Some few of the girls, after leaving school, go out as domestic servants either in local situations or to England or Scotland.

Both sexes usually marry young, the matches being arranged by the parents, and money rather than romance being the chief element in the case, as a projected marriage is often abandoned owing to disputes between parents without the young people themselves being consulted in the matter. Love-making, except in the case of engaged couples, but seldom occurs, but that it does sometimes happen is shown by the number and variety of love-charms and omens. As in most other parts of Ireland the majority of marriages occur before Shrove. When full agreements have been made by the parents, the young man goes and asks the girl personally. If he be refused, he does not, like an Inishbofin man, consider himself disgraced, nor is he inconsolable.

Engaged couples or newly married people often come in for an amount of attention from the children of the neighbourhood, which, however flattering it may be, is decidedly embarrassing; they are followed about and cheered whenever they appear together. Weddings are occasions of family festivities, and are usually followed by a dance. "Straw-boys" go round to the house on these occasions and take part in the dancing. They are disguised in tall conical-shaped straw masks, adorned with strips of red and green cloth, white shirts decorated with coloured ribbons, and white or red petticoats. The band is headed by a captain and a mate, who enter the house first and declare that they are shipwrecked sailors, and that they have come to dance at the wedding; the captain then dances with the bride, the mate with the bridesmaid, and the rest of the band with the other girls. It is usual to treat the straw-boys to drink, but they often refuse it, and never demand money, or indulge in any rowdy conduct.

The young couple usually set up house on their own account, except in the case of the youngest son, who inherits his parents' house and property, in which case the bride goes to live with her people-in-law.

When a person is dying, windows and doors are thrown open, and the clock (if there be one) stopped; it is considered unlucky or improper for any of those in the house to cry until after the death has actually occured.

Wakes are still held in this district, and many of the old observances and games are kept up; but owing to the discouragement of these by the clergy, the people show a great reluctance to give any information on the matter. A good deal of drinking usually takes place on these occasions.

The funeral customs have undergone some change during the past thirty years, but much still remains that is worthy of notice. A grave is not usually dug until the coffin reaches the graveyard, if begun before hand it is never dug on a Monday, or commenced at least, but a start is made, if necessity compels, by raising a few sods on Sunday. It is believed to be unlucky to bury a corpse on New Year's Day, an act which is thought to bring misfortune to the whole neighbourhood.

The coffin is usually taken out the back door of the house, and conveyed to the cemetery by the longest route. At the graveyard the *caoine* is raised by the women immediately after the religious ceremony is concluded. The burial grounds are kept much better than in many other parts of the West; and on Inishkea, as well as in the Mullet, it it is customary to decorate the graves with large white pebbles, and to place at the head a neatly made wooden cross. A curious custom exists, some instances of which were observed at Tarmoncarra, of placing tobacco pipes on the graves; these are the pipes which were left unused after the wake. What the reason is for so placing them could not be ascertained, but it is considered extremely unlucky to remove them.

Unbaptised infants are interred in separate burying grounds by themselves, several of which are in the district.

It is now no longer customary for the people of the Mullet to bury their dead in Inisglora, the last instance of this having occured over thirty years ago. Formerly many families used regularly to make use of this island as a cemetery, always taking a body over from a point of the mainland opposite, which was stated by tradition to have once been connected with the main, but to have got separated afterwards by a channel which has gradually widened.

Maxwell,[1] writing in 1832, says—"There are no people on earth more punctilious in the interment of their dead than the peasantry of this remote district. A strange and unaccountable custom exists of burying different families resident on the main in island cemeteries, and great difficulty and often great danger attends the conveyance of a corpse to its insulated resting place. No inducement will make these wild people inter a body apart from the tomb of its fathers, and, if a boat will live, the corpse will be transported to the family tomb. At times the weather renders this impracticable, but the deceased is kept for many days unburied in the hope that the storm may subside; and only when frail mortality evinces unequivocal tokens of decay will the relatives consent to unite its dust with the ashes of a stranger."

A considerable number of migratory labourers leave this district annually to do harvesting work in England, on the proceeds of which work they in part support themselves during the winter. The number doing thus has decreased somewhat of late years.

There is not much to be said about the everyday mode of life. The men fish and attend to their holdings; the women manage household affairs and assist at field work in times of pressure. The people are early risers in the summer months, and, as a rule, retire to bed early, few lights being seen in the hamlets after nine or ten p.m.

---

[1] Maxwell, W. H., "Wild sports of the West," chap. xix.

A cruel custom is said to have been common in the district at one time, which was still in use in 1835, of harrowing with the harrow fastened to the horses tail.

The females of a family sleep in the " room," the men in the bed in the kitchen; if the family be large, the beds will be very full, the occupants lying "heads and points," as several of my informants phrased it, that is, some with their heads in the ordinary place, others with theirs to the foot of the bed. No night-clothing is worn by either sex among the poorer people.

A method of sleeping when the house was much crowded was formerly practised in this district, which is fully described by a writer[1] who has been frequently quoted in this Report :—" This is what is called sleeping in *stradoge*, and *is regulated* as follows :—The floor is thickly strewed with fresh rushes, and stripping themselves entirely, the whole family lie down at once and together, covering themselves with blankets if they have them, if not, with their day-clothing, but they lie down *decently*, and in order; the eldest daughter next the wall farthest from the door, then all the sisters according to their ages ; next the mother, father, and sons in succession, and then the strangers, whether the travelling pedlar, or tailor, or beggar; thus the strangers are kept aloof from the female part of the family, and if there be apparent community, there is great propriety of conduct."

3. *Food.*—The dietary varies somewhat with the locality, but fish seems to form a considerable part of it in all but the mountainous portions of the district. Flesh or fowl are rarely tasted, except at Christmas time, or at Michaelmas, or some other great occasion. The islanders are said to make some use of sea birds, but use fish as the staple animal food. This is eaten fresh in summer, and coarsely salted for winter use.

The main articles of diet are stirabout, soda-bread, and boxty (a form of damper made of grated raw potatoes, and cooked on a griddle. This extremely indigestible form of bread is much used in the mountainous parts), potatoes, and tea, which is becoming more extensively used than formerly, and is now taken at nearly every meal. Whatever the other meals may be composed of, fish forms part of supper.

An average day's dietary in the Mullet would be somewhat as follows :—

Breakfast.—Potatoes and fish, or Indian meal (sometimes oatmeal) stirabout, buttermilk.

---

[1] C. O., " Sketches in Erris and Tyrawley," p. 34.

Dinner.—Tea and soda-bread, or fish and potatoes.

Supper.—Fish and potatoes, with buttermilk as a beverage, or stirabout and milk.

In the mountainous parts, potatoes and stirabout form, with tea and boxty, the larger part of the dietary. In this region also the poorer families do not usually take more than two meals a day during the winter months.

Butter, cheese, and eggs are but very little used, the eggs being exported, and in some remote parts sometimes bartered to the small dealers for tea, sugar, or tobacco, instead of being sold for money.

In many parts a good deal of poteen is consumed, as illicit distilling, though much less common than formerly, still prevails to a considerable extent.

4. *Clothing.*—When seen in their holiday dress the people appear to be well dressed, and almost over-clothed; but the everyday working-dress is, among the poorer part of the population, often of a very nondescript, not to say ragged, character.

At first sight there does not seem to be much homespun worn, but on closer inspection a great deal of it appears to be still in use, but to be made up in modern style. It is usually dyed blue, but a good deal of it is a natural grey made by mixing black and white wool, and which, as it does not fade, is much in use. The costume of the men varies much; the old swallow-tailed coat with the metal buttons is now seldom seen, being replaced by more modern patterns. The trousers are either homespun or corduroy. Hats and caps of all shapes are worn; they are usually purchased in Belmullet from local shopkeepers who import them. Many of the men, on working days, wear shirts of a thick, white, homespun flannel.

The men of Inishkea still retain a distinctive attire, their dress being composed of a navy-blue homespun, of which shirt, vest, and trousers are made; many wear a loose blouse or frock of the same material, which they prefer to "shop cloth," as they say it is warmer, wears longer, and stands sea water better; it is certainly more picturesque.

A great deal of second hand clothing is sold on fair days to the poorer class of people by "Cheap Jacks," who dispose of their wares by a sort of Dutch auction.

The men wear boots in every-day dress, but the women and children do so only on Sundays, market-days, and holidays. It is a common custom for women going to market in Belmullet to walk barefooted, carrying their boots in their baskets until they reach the outskirts of the town, where they sit down by the roadside, and put on their boots and stockings, taking them off again when starting for home.

The old-fashioned frock or kilt-shaped garment, made of red or grey homespun, and buttoned up the back, is still worn by boys up to twelve years of age.

The dress of the women is on the whole less changed than that of the men. Many of the elderly women wear the white-frilled cap, others have a small red kerchief tied under the chin. Over the shoulders a shawl of tartan or other striking pattern is folded, but this is not so frequently of a bright red, as in other districts, as the darker colours seem to be more in favour; beneath the shawl is a boddice of some dark material. The petticoat is short, but is only occasionally the typical red homespun of the western peasant. It is often grey, or dyed purple, blue, or some other bright colour, and is sometimes ornamented by a few rows of black braid. Aprons of check are much worn. Many of the older women wear the heavy blue cloak with cape and hood on Sundays and holidays. The younger women to a large extent copy modern fashions on festive occasions, but the result is not happy, as their taste in colours is curious, and they certainly look better in native costume.

A great variety of homespuns are made in the district, there being several weavers who turn out coarse flannel, tweeds, and friezes, some of which are very good specimens of hand-loom work. The dyes are nearly all imported, indigo and the made-up aniline dyes being most used. Purple loosestrife (*Lythrum salicaria*), which was at one time pretty generally employed for this purpose, is now only used for dying stockings.

5. *Dwellings.*—The habitations of the people present considerable variety, some being extremely poor, others of a fairly good class. The description given below applies solely to the houses of the people of the rural parts, and not to Belmullet (which is a cleanly and well-built little town, composed almost entirely of good-slated houses of two stories) nor to the houses of the proprietors or large holders.

Of late years there has been much improvement in the style of dwelling, but few indeed of the old turf cabins remain; while the semi-subterranean huts, some of which were inhabited in 1841, have become altogether extinct.

The *Parliamentary Gazetteer* (1846) describes the majority of dwellings as being built partly of stone and partly of turf, and consisting of only one or at most two rooms.

An average dwelling now is built of stone, sometimes dry, at others cemented by "dobe" or tempered clay, or sometimes mortar. It generally consists of two apartments, the kitchen and the "room." The kitchen, which is usually of pretty large size, is used as the living room ; it has a floor of beaten clay. This room has one, or perhaps, two windows of small size, and seldom made to open. These are always glazed now-a-days, but in the last century they were covered with oiled sheepskin. The house has two doors, both of which open directly into the kitchen, and are situated about two-thirds of the way from the partition wall of the two apartments.

The end of the kitchen farthest from the fire is used as a pen for the cattle and pigs. The fowl roost where they can, often on the backs of the cattle.

Above the beams or couples in this part of the kitchen boards are sometimes placed, making a sort of loft, in which fishing and boat tackle, agricultural implements, and other articles are stored.

The fireplace is built against the partition wall between the kitchen and the room. It consists of a stone hearth backed by a "hob," also of stone, built out slantwise behind it to make the fire draw well. This class of house has no chimney, the smoke escaping through a circular hole in the roof immediately above the hearth.

"The room" is a smaller apartment than the kitchen, (measuring about 12 feet by 10 feet) it has one or two small windows, and the floor is sometimes boarded.

The furniture of the house is poor and scanty, that of the kitchen consisting of a bedstead, rudely made up of drift-wood, two posts being driven into the floor, a longitudinal piece uniting these and two cross-beams at head and foot resting by one end on the posts, and having the other built into the wall. Sometimes it is built up into four-poster shape and has curtains. The bedding is composed either of feather ticks, or, with the poorer people, of straw, covered with coarse sacking. The bedclothes are often very dirty. There is a dresser covered with earthenware plates, cups, and jugs of a poor and cheap description, a table, two or three chairs, and a couple of forms or settles. A long straw rope is usually stretched across the apartment to hang clothes to dry on. Worsted when spun, nets, &c., are hung from the couples.

"The room" contains one or two beds of the sort described, a chair or two, a table (in some cases), and a large chest.

The domestic utensils consist of the usual three-legged pot, a griddle, a gridiron, and sometimes a pot oven, a few staved wooden piggins, a boran or sheepskin sieve, and, in the mountains and islands, a quern, now only used usually for grinding barley for cattle food,

though it may be put to the less innocent purpose of preparing malt
for poteen, and a spinning-wheel of the usual type. For light at night
modern lamps are coming into use, but in many houses the "flare" is
used. It consists of a rude sconce, in which is fastened a cylindrical
reservoir for oil, closed at the top by a lid, and having a spout like
that of a coffee-pot, through which the wick is drawn. Rush lights
are still used by some.

The house is often whitewashed outside; the roof is thatch, of
straw in most localities, but on the islands, and some places in the
peninsula, bent is use instead. This is laid on over "scraws" of grass-
turf and fastened down by sougans (straw ropes), the ends of which
may be attached to pegs driven into the walls, or have long pieces of
wood or heavy stones fastened to them. These ropes are often arranged
in a net work so as to hold the thatch more securely. Coir rope, bought
in Belmullet, is now used by some instead of sougans. The gable is
stepped or cut away so that the thatch does not project over the end wall.

There are several other types of houses, though the style just
described is the most common. Most of the newer houses and those
building have chimneys, pig-styes of turf or stone, and in some cases
byres. Few of the old one-roomed dwellings, built partly or altogether of turf, are still to be seen, but there are a number of one-
roomed huts of stone, many of which have no windows.

The most primitive habitations in the district, and perhaps in
Ireland, are the rude huts (*boolies*) on Inishglora, inhabited during the
lobster fishing season by the men of Inishkea; they are about a dozen
in number, rudely built of dry stone and thatched with "scraws."
There is not room to stand upright in them, the height from floor to
roof being about 5 feet. Internally they contain a rude bunk filled with
straw for sleeping in and a few large stones to sit upon. Cooking
appears to be done out of doors. Successive batches of men live in
these huts for about three months of the year. Some of the poorest
houses on the mainland are in the isolated and primitive village of
Fallmore, where few of the dwellings have windows and few or none
chimneys. The houses on the islands are decidedly among the best in
the district. Many are whitewashed inside, and the furniture is of a
superior class, abundant material being thrown up as drift wood. The
beds are four-posted structures, with flat board tops, and some of them
have bright-coloured curtains, and the bedding is clean and tidy-
looking.

6. *Transport.*—Lying as it does far from towns of any size, and
separated from the nearest by a wide stretch of wild and thinly-

populated country, the district under consideration is practically isolated, and communication with other parts of the country is carried on by road or by sea. Mails and passengers are carried daily to and from Ballina and Belmullet by a good two-horse (Bianconi) stage-car; and a similar vehicle, an opposition venture, also makes the journey daily with passengers and light goods. The country beyond Belmullet is provided with mails twice weekly. Goods are conveyed by carts from Ballina, a distance of over forty miles, during the winter and spring, and large sailing boats are sometimes employed carrying heavy goods from Westport. But few wheeled-vehicles are used except by the better-to-do, and in the remoter parts hardly any are employed, turf, sea-weed, &c., being carried in cleaves or pardoges (panniers with movable bottoms, slung over the backs of horses or donkeys). The people, if poor, have to walk; those better off may ride to market. It is common for two to ride the one horse, a man in the saddle and a woman *en croupe*, or both equestrians may be women, in which case, sometimes, but very rarely, the woman in front may ride astride.

The main roads are pretty good, but many of the smaller ones are very little used, except at harvest time or when turf is being got in, and as a result are grass-grown and uneven. Some small fishing hamlets and outlying places are still unprovided with roads.

For water transport there are the sailing boats before mentioned, used for the conveyance of goods from Westport. The form of boat most in use is the curragh, which is manned by three men; it varies somewhat in pattern in different localities.

In the Mullet and the islands 142 curraghs are in use. Very few boats of other patterns are kept, as there are only three second-class boats (yawls), and about thirty third-class. At Portacloy there are about 30 curraghs.

The southern part of the peninsula and the islands obtain their turf supply by boat from Achill and Ballycroy.

V.—FOLK-LORE.

Although poor in so many other respects, Erris is particularly rich in folk-lore, many old customs, traditions, and beliefs, which have died out, or are dying elsewhere, still flourishing there. The legends and tales of the past and many old songs are still current, especially among the older people, who, however, will not readily communicate them to strangers, so that only a resident well acquainted with Irish is likely to succeed in collecting much. Fortunately there is a resident (the Rev. P. A. O'Reilly), who is engaged in collecting the old Irish songs of the district, several of which he has already published. As to the legends, many of these have been recorded by C. O. and Mr. Knight, to whose works the reader is referred.

The following notes, mainly dealing with what may be termed minor folk-lore, were some of them obtained from fishermen and others of the natives, but mainly through the kindness of several residents, some of whom desired that their names should not be mentioned.

1. *Customs and Beliefs.*—For the majority of the notes on these I am indebted to the kindness of Mr. J. A. Nolan, of Belmullet, who, being a native of the district, and personally acquainted with nearly everyone in it, has an exceptionally large knowledge of the subject; for a large part of what remains I have also to thank Messrs. F. C. Wallace, D.I. R.I.C., Belmullet, and P. T. O'Reilly, Carn.

A very large number of things are considered lucky or the reverse. It is unlucky to dig a grave on a Monday, on which day also no change of residence should be made, a Friday should rather be chosen, as that is the lucky day for moving. To meet a red-haired woman on starting out in the morning, to mention a priest while fishing, to take fish out of a house without sprinkling some salt on it, to sell milk without putting in a pinch of salt, to give fire out of the house on May-day, or to anyone in whose dwelling a sick person may be, all these are unlucky. People "born with teeth" are unlucky also; but to be "born with a caul" is a sign of great good fortune, though should the original owner ever see it his luck will depart; the possession of a caul is believed to protect against death by drowning. A mole on the face, if "above the breath," is considered to have the same protective influence.

Death within the year is believed to be the fate of the man who has the temerity to make an addition to the western side of his house, or to build out at the back; several instances of men who died within a short time after thus offending are sure to be told to the incredulous.

The banshee, the death-watch, the creaking of furniture, and the howling of a dog at night are all looked upon as death-warnings. Several persons were met with who asserted that they had heard the banshee before the death of relatives.

At weddings the bride and bridegroom must step over the threshold of the chapel door together, as whichever goes out first will be the first to die.

The effect of the evil eye is much dreaded, and illness and misfortune are ascribed to it ; for this reason, a child or an animal should not be praised without saying " God bless it," to avert misfortune. To counteract this influence, human beings may be spit upon, or the sign of the cross made on them in the name of the Trinity. Cattle sometimes have knot-charms tied to their tails.

Many animals have beliefs or customs connected with them. A fox should not be interfered with by the people in his neighbourhood, or he will revenge himself by raids on their fowls ; if well treated he will do no damage.

Seals are thought by some to be enchanted men or transmigrated souls, and for this reason are not molested. A man at Portacloy asserted that it was unlucky to kill seals, and added, as a warning, that he knew a man, a relative of his own, who went into a cave to slay a seal, and on raising his club to strike it, saw the animal change into a large frog. He did not, however, seem to have any very great faith in his own story, as a few minutes afterwards he offered to sell a sealskin.

It is believed also that on some nights seals assume human shape, and that a number of them gather together on the rocks and wail aloud.

C. O. states that the people of Tip were reputed by their neighbours to be " peculiar " because they ate seals' flesh.

The soil of Inishglora is thought to be so fatal to rats that if one of these animals be brought to the island it will die as soon as it touches the soil, and a handful of sand from the island will perfectly protect a house against this kind of vermin. A black hen used, on some occasions (and may perhaps be still) to be buried alive with its wings spread out to bring about a fair wind or some desired good fortune.

Ghosts and apparitions are fully believed in. Two instances of the spirits of drowned persons being seen walking about are reported to have occurred within the past year; one of these was said to have occurred near Blacksod, where the ghost of a sailor was seen on the sea-shore. An apparition in the form of a black dog is sometimes seen by belated travellers not far from Portacloy. About half-a-mile outside Belmullet and within the peninsula of the Mullet, there is a mound in a field by the roadside; this is raised over the bodies of some of the peasantry who were slain in a combat with the yeomanry (known as the battle of Meenane Creve), in the year 1793. At this spot the ghost of a young man without a head is seen sitting upon the bank by the roadside; after a time it rises, walks across the road to the mound, and then vanishes.

The ghost of Major —— is reported to be sometimes seen riding a phantom horse at a spot near Carn, and circles on the grass are pointed out as marking the scene of his equestrian feats; he is also said to ride at times to Bingham Castle.

There is a strong belief in fairies, and many people are to be found who say that they have seen them. They are said to dance at night and cause fairy rings; they dwell in grassy mounds and travel from place to place, using stems of the ragweed as horses.

The mirage which is sometimes seen off the coast is ascribed to the fairies if it assumes the appearance of boats or ships; they are believed to have been seen to land on the shore, haul up their boats, and vanish. Many stories are told respecting the impudent pranks of these beings, and to their revenge for some injury, disease in man and cattle is sometimes ascribed. A man may become paralysed or waste away and die from fairy influence as well as from the evil eye, but their malice may have a less serious ending, and may only produce some disfigurement. Some time ago a man was one day walking homewards, when he saw lying on the road a bright new razor; he picked it up and took it home with him, but after shaving with it got *sycosis menti*, and the implement was then declared to be a "fairy razor."

Women dying in puerperal fever are believed to have been taken by the fairies to act as wet-nurses, and infants may be "taken away," and changelings put in their places. The changeling may be got rid of by putting on a roaring fire and throwing him behind it, when he at once vanishes in the smoke. The *ignus fatuus* is believed to be caused by the fairies to lead people astray.

The attentions of these creatures are not expended on human beings alone, for they may revenge themselves on those who vex them by attacking domestic animals. Cattle becoming ill suddenly are supposed to be "shot" by the fairies, and the owners will often go to a great deal of trouble to find a person who possess a "fairy stone," which is the only remedy. These stones are treasured very carefully and are kept wrapped up in a piece of cloth; they are used by rubbing them on the afflicted animal, and repeating a charm or prayer. Unfortunately no specimen of these stones was seen, so it cannot be stated positively whether they are flint arrow-heads or not.

A farm-house at a place called Illaunglass, in the Mullet, has a tale connected with it, illustrating the causing of disease in cattle by the fairies. A few years ago the cattle on this farm became ill, and one after another died ; the people of the house consulted a " fairy woman," who told them that the cause of the disease was the defiling of the fairies play-ground, by allowing a manure heap on the south side of the house, but that if this were removed that all would be well. Her advice was taken, and from that day forth the illness ceased. Dirty water should not be thrown out at night for fear of offending the fairies.

Many of the old customs mentioned by writers of the earlier part of the century have become extinct. People from the mainland no longer bury their dead on Inishglora, and some other customs connected with this island have died out since it became uninhabited ; the first that two people could not go together into one of the ruined cells or cloghans without breaking bread between them, neglect of which would cause one of the two to die within the year ; the other that every visitor should kiss the wooden statute of St. Brendan.[1] Though these customs have gone, many still continue to exist—wakes, funeral customs, and straw-boys at weddings have been already mentioned ; wren hunting is practised, and the " wran-bush " carried round on St. Stephen's Day, as in most other parts of Ireland. On St. John's Eve bon-fires, or Beltain fires, are lighted, and people used to jump through the smoke over them when they got low ; many still endeavour on these occasions to take home a live coal to kindle their own fires with.

The sign of the cross is made over the mouth when yawning to avert evil. Hair-cuttings are carefully put away in a hole in the wall in order that strength may be preserved.

The sale of cattle is completed by dipping a stick in dirt, and marking the beasts therewith.

Girls sometimes try means of discovering what their future husband will be like. The following is a specimen :—On the first sight of the first new moon of the New Year, the girl kneels down and says seven " Our Fathers " and seven " Hail Marys " ; then she takes some of the clay from under her left knee and puts it into a left stocking, which she then buries until retiring at night, when she takes it up and sleeps on it to dream of her future husband.

There is a love charm of a rather gruesome character which is still

---

[1] It used to be the custom for all ships passing Inishglora to lower top sails in honour of St. Brendan ; and it was believed that any man who thrice lifted the statue in his arms was rendered capable of helping women in difficult labours.— O'Donovan.

believed in, or at least spoken of, though not practised. It is called the spancel, and is thus described by C. O.[1] :—"This spancel, called in Irish 'stheioul dhrum agus tharragh,' signifying the skin of the back and of the belly, consists of a continuous band of skin taken from round the length of the body, viz. from the side of one foot up the outside of that leg and side, over the head and down the other side to the sole of the other foot, up the inside of that leg and down the inside of the other, until the stripe meets where it first set out ; it is used as a love charm, and its power is believed to be irresistible, it being only necessary in order to secure the affections of the victim, to tie the spancel round him while asleep ; if he does not awake during the operation all *must* turn out to the wish of the operator ; if he does awake, he dies before the end of the year, so the poor desired one has no escape." The same author mentions several instances of this, which were said to have occurred shortly before he wrote (1841), one of which, the discovery of three young women taking the spancel off a corpse, is still remembered by some of the older inhabitants. There are several holy wells in the district, but the most famous is the well of St. Brendan, on Inishglora, the water of which is said to remain sweet and pure if drawn by a man, but to turn bloody and become full of worms if a woman has the temerity to take it. Many tales are told of the misfortunes which have happened to women who persisted in drawing water from this well after being warned. There is now resident in Belmullet an old man who lived for some years on Inishglora. This man solemnly declared to the Rev. P. O'Reilly and the writer that he had three times cleared out the well after women had taken water from it, and that on each occasion it was "full of blood and corruption"; he also said that from the time he began to clean out the well until the job was completed no water flowed in, though it began to come as soon as the cleansing was finished. He added that if a woman were left alone on the island with only a male child of a month old, and she wanted to get water, the vessel would have to be held by the child's hand to prevent the water from becoming bloody.

2. *Charms and Leechcraft.*—Disease is often ascribed to supernatural agencies, and for this reason is often treated by charms or incantations. There are several local " wise " men and women who treat disorders partly by means of charms, partly by herbal and animal remedies. In some cases the idea underlying the treatment

---

[1] "Erris and Tyrawley," p. 90.

seems to be the transferrence of the malady to some inanimate object, which, if found, may transmit the disease to the finder.

Charms, &c.—For "the Rose" (erysipelas) the following is sometimes made use of, but to be efficacious it is thought that it must always be applied by a person of the opposite sex to the patient :—

The operator rubs salt butter into the part affected, and prays over it, this process being repeated twice a week. (Communicated by a friend, who has seen it employed.)

For the same—the old woman who performs this takes ten pebbles from a well or brook, one she throws back into the water, the other nine she takes to the patient, and having muttered some prayers over them she puts each down on its upper side (*i.e.* the side prayed over, and taking them up one by one, she rubs them on the affected part in the name of the Trinity, and of the *King of the Rose.* She then takes the stones to a stream and throws them in, praying that so and so (naming the patient) may never have "the rose" so long as the stones remain there.

The following is employed for a mote or piece of barley beard in the eye. The woman who practises this takes a clean bowl and a jug or cup full of clear water, she rinses her mouth with the water until it ceases to be sullied, when she takes a fresh quantity in her mouth and holds it there until she has repeated, or is supposed to repeat, some prayer or charm. She then empties her mouth into the clean vessel, and shows the mote floating in it.[1] Written charms for the toothache are sometimes worn about the person.

For a headache "head measuring" is employed; several old woman practise it. The cause of the pain is believed to be the opening of the head by separation of the bones. To cure this state of affairs. the woman takes a cord which she passes round the head, and marks the length ; this done she mutters a charm or prayer and measures again, showing the patient that the circumference is now less and that the head is closed, a kerchief is usually kept bound around the brows for some time afterwards to prevent recurrence of the pain. There is great faith in the efficacy of the touch of a seventh son, especially in "evil" and ringworm. An Inishkea fisherman stated that on the islands it is believed that toothache may be completely removed and will never return if the tooth be rubbed with a dead man's finger.

---

[1] I am indebted to the kindness of the Rev. H. Hewson, P.P., Belmullet, for the description of these two charms both of which he has seen performed.

In cases of difficult labour a ploughman may be called in to lift and shake the woman gently, which it is thought will produce the desired effect. The reason given is that as he shakes and scatters the seed on the earth, so also he ought to produce a good effect here.

A nail which has got into the foot is always thrown into the fire.

Leechcraft.—Though regular medical assistance is usually sought for serious complaints, yet, the more common ailments are often treated by the people themselves, several of the older men and women enjoying some local celebrity for this.

The following list of substances used medicinally was collected; it is believed to be but a small fraction of the local pharmacopœia.

(A.) Animal substances.—Saliva is used for many purposes; thus button scurvy is treated by spitting on the floor and rubbing on the mixed saliva and dust with the right thumb.

Seal oil is rubbed in for sprains and rheumatism, for which it has a great reputation locally; it is sold in Belmullet at a pretty high price.

The tongue of a fox is used as a poultice to extract thorns, &c.

(B.) Herbs.—Mr. Nolan kindly provided the following list of plants in use in the district, most of which he has seen used. The qualities of many of these were also described to me by several of the country people.

Dandelion (*Leoontodon taraxacum*), used for "liver troubles."

Comfrey (*Symphytum officinale*), used as a styptic.

Samphire (*Crithmum maritimum*), used, boiled in milk, for heart-burn.

Self-heal (locally called Heartsease) (*Brunella vulgaris*), used for palpitations.

Mountain sage (*Teucrium scorodonia*), used "for the heart" and in cough mixtures.

Ground-wood, or Bog-bark (not identified), used for gravel (boiled in milk).

Bugloss (*Echium* or *Lycopsis*), used, in poultices with oat-meal, for abscesses, &c.

Ground-ivy (*Nepeta glechoma*), used, as a "tea," for "heart beat," or mixed with other herbs for a cough.

Nettles (*Urtica dioica*), used, with ginger, for "wind on the stomach."

Ivy (*Hedera helix*), leaves used as a cap for a "scabby head."

Burdock root (*Arctium lappa*),
Furze tops (*Ulex*),
Broom (*Cytisus scoparius*),
Carageen moss (*Sphærococcus europæus*),
} usually combined and boiled with sugar-stick to form a cough-syrup.

Horehound (*Marrubium vulgare*), used as an expectorant.

Marsh-mallow (*Althæa officinalis*), used as poultice for "sore breast."

Mullein (*Verbascum thapsus*), used as an infusion for coughs.

Parsley (*Petroselinum sativum*), boiled in milk for "gravel."

Belladonna (*Atropa belladonna*), used for palpitation or "heart beat."

It will be seen from this list that several of the remedies used are officinal; and others, though not officially recognised, possess medicinal properties.

3. *Legends and Traditions.*—There are many of these current in the district, but only a small number could be collected. Among all these, few bearing on the early history of this region seem to have come down to the present time, except the tradition of a great battle fought at Cross, in the Mullet, between the people of the country, and an invading army under a king of Munster who was slain in the fight, and over whose remains a tumulus was erected.

There is, so far as could be ascertained, no tradition as to the origin of the earlier inhabitants, either of the mainland, or of the islands; but the families whose ancestors came from Ulster two centuries ago are well known, and sometimes are called by the name Ultagh, instead of their own surnames.

It would be expected that there would be some tales connected with the duns, of which there are several, but very few seem to be known, even the oldest inhabitants not seeming to have heard any history of them. The story of Dun Donald, related by Knight,[1] the vague tradition that Dunamoa was built by the Burkes, and besieged by the "Danes"; and another concerning Dun Fiachrach, which is believed to have been a favourite resting place for the children of Lir, and the fishermen of the neighbourhood say that the founder of the fort used to ride a "water-horse," on which he could leap across the deep caves on to the cliffs on each side of the dun. Many of the people ascribe these forts to "the Danes."

The favourite tales and poems are either ancient myth, or of a semi-religious character; legends of the saints forming a large portion of the old chroniclers' stock.

Mr Knight says[2]—"It is not from these cairns (Seefins) alone we claim Fingal and Ossian as *peculiarly* ours; we have heard them in *real song*, and many a winter's evening have I heard the old chronicler lying on his back quietly, in the bed beyond the fire, repeat the

---

[1] P. Knight, Erris, &c., p. 166. [2] *Ibid.*, p. 110.

'deed of old' to delighted listening ears, but in language so ancient as to be now almost unintelligible to most Irish speakers of the modern school." The tradition of St. Brendan's discovery of America is well known, but the statement made by old writers about the supposed anti-putrefactive nature of the soil of Inishglora, does not seem to be recognised by the people of the district, who point to the bones among the ruins in disproof of the story.

O'Flaherty, in his "Ogygia," mentions the island in the following lines :—

> " In Innisglore on Erris shore,
> Should we the bodies of our sires explore
> We'ed find them blooming, fresh and fair,
> No human flesh can rot or perish there."

The Priest's Leap.—Just below the sea face of Dunnamoe, and separated from it by a narrow channel, is a large rock, which, tradition relates, was once part of the cliff on which the fort is built. It is said that once in the old times, some say the time of Cromwell, a priest was saying Mass at Tarmoncarra, when he was surprised by the soldiery. Not knowing whither to fly, he ran towards the cliffs and reached them at this spot, his pursuers coming close behind him. Just when all seemed lost the large mass of rock on which he was broke away from the cliff and settled down in the sea as an islet, bearing down the priest with it, comfortably seated, in a niche, known as the "priest's chair," sheltered from the bullets of his enemies. Thus protected he remained until night, when he was taken off in a curragh by his people. The place has since been known as the "Priest's Leap."

The Namhoge or Neewoge.—There was formerly on Iniskea a small stone figure called the *neewoge* (little saint), which was believed to have great power over the weather, and was accordingly treated with great reverence and used to be invoked for favourable winds. It is said that a pirate landed on the island, and after carrying off all that was portable, set fire to the houses, with the exception of the one in which the *neewoge* was kept, which did not take fire. Search was made for the cause and the image was taken out and broken. The *neewoge* never fully recovered this treatment. His power, though still great, was not the same as it had been.

Some years ago the attention of the parish priest became directed to the existence of this image, and having obtained the stone by a stratagem from the woman who was its custodian he threw it into the sea. As he died not very long after this, some of the islanders ascribe his death to his interference with this figure. An Inishkea man spoke about the matter with much indignation even after the lapse of years, and said that they had never known misfortune or hunger in the island until after the distruction of this *neewoge.*

Many different accounts have been given of the image itself. One writer (C. O.) states that it was a stone figure of rude workmanship, and that it was dressed in a suit of homespun, renewed every year.

The description given by those who have seen it agree in stating that it was not a statue but a small flat stone. One informant believed it to be part of the head of a stone figure. This was enveloped in a small bag of homespun, which was replaced when it got old and soiled, and was kept in a blind window or recess in the wall in one of the houses.

St. Brendan and the Devil.—During my visit to Inishglora some of the Inishkea fishermen, who were camped there at the time, pointed out that no grass grew on a part of the island, and gave the following explanation :—St. Brendan was one day disturbed in his devotions by the devil, who appeared to him in the form of a beautiful girl and tempted him. The saint indignantly repulsed the temptress, and drove her towards the end of the island, blessing the soil as he went, but at the point where the grass ends, Satan changed his form and assumed the shape of a ram, which so astonished the saint that in his excitement he ceased blessing and gave chase to the evil one who ran to the rocks and jumped into the sea. The unblessed land is that on which the grass does not grow.

VI. Archæology.

The few notes made in this section do not purport to be fully descriptive, but merely to indicate the nature of the antiquities of the region, which are of importance in the study of the people as bearing on the history of their past, and to direct the attention of archaeologists to the quantity of material worthy of study and record which is still to be met with in this part of county Mayo.

1. *Survivals.*—The district is comparatively rich in these, though many articles in use in the localities previously reported on are now quite extinct in Erris. The primitive condition of many of the houses, the absence of chimneys, and the custom of taking cattle into the dwellings have already been referred to.

The quern is still in use in several houses, especially on the islands and in the remoter localities, though now only employed for grinding barley for cattle food, or in some few cases for malt for *poteen*.

Hooped piggins are used in many houses, as also are sheepskin sieves (*borans*).

The spinning-wheel for wool is of the usual Connaught type, without treadle, and is made in the district. The cards used for the wool are imported, being all made in Dublin. The hand-looms are the same as used elsewhere in the West, and of rather rude construction, though capable of turning out good work.

A machine of rather primitive design is used for compressing cloth. It was made by its user, and has been working for many years.

Rush-lights are used in some houses, and in others the rude lamp already referred to, which is evidently merely a reproduction in tin-ware of the old stone or iron lamp for fish oil.

The stills employed by the makers of poteen are constructed of tin, and of simple but effective design. They are made in the owners houses by tinkers.

The curragh, of the usual form, is the boat most in use, and seems likely to hold its own. It is now covered with tarred canvas, but seventy years ago horse-skins were used for this purpose. A large stone is often used as an anchor for small boats.

2. *Antiquities* may be divided into two classes—(*a*) Architectural remains, and (*b*) Articles of use or ornament. (*a*) Architectural remains are still very numerous, though many of the most interesting have altogether disappeared; of these the most noticeable was the *Oileach*, the fortified seat of the chiefs of Hy-Fiachrach, which was situated at Elly in the Mullet, on or near the position of Bingham's Castle. Several castles belonging to the Barrets and Burkes have also been entirely destroyed.

Some of the ruins still remaining are of pagan origin, others are ecclesiastical structures. The principal pagan antiquities are the duns or forts, both stone and earthen, the monuments, &c. There are several duns, both within the district actually treated of in this Paper, and along the coast line of the surrounding country; those within the Mullet are *Dunnamoe*, a stone fort of large size, built on a rocky promontory overhanging the sea, and formerly one of the most perfect on this coast; of late years, however, it has suffered severely, the greater part of the wall has been broken down to afford building material for houses and walls about Belmullet; the guard-chambers mentioned by O'Donovan and others are now almost destroyed, the outworks thrown down. One part of the wall alone is perfect, that overhanging the sea on the south side. Where the original wall-face shows it is like the forts of Aran, composed of blocks of stone, fitted neatly together without mortar; it is about ten feet high and eight feet in thickness. The ground in front of the wall was originally provided with a fosse and a wide belt of stone-stakes fixed upright in the earth, as in Dun Ængus on Inishmore, Aran; but all of these, with the exception of a few stumps, have now disappeared. A full description of this fort is given by O'Donovan in his MS. letters to the Ordnance Survey. The name of this fort, Dunnamoe, is now believed by the people to be *Dun-na-mbo*, or the fort of the cows, a name, the origin of which is stated in a MS. letter[1] by a Mr. Owen Heenaghan, of Emlybeg, in the Mullet, dated May, 1821. to be explained by the local tradition, that the cattle of the people were kept there at the time of the battle at Cross, to be afterwards referred to. O'Donovan, however, believed it to have been originally named *Dun Modha*, after Modha, a chief of the Clann Huamore, Belgae, who also gave his name to Inis Modha, or the Clew Bay Islands.

The other forts are *Dun Fiachra*, which consists of an earthen wall across the narrowest part of the neck of a long narrow peninsula, with precipitous coast, situated in the townland of Aghadoon; the remains of a stone doon, "Spinkadoon," of somewhat larger area, are situated a short distance to the north of this fort. *Dunadearg*, the fort of the red man, is also situated on the west coast of the Mullet. *Porth*, an earthen dun situated near the rectory, is barely traceable. *Dunavinalla*, a large fort, stands on a rocky height just outside the inlet of Portacloy.

There are several monuments of early date, the most remarkable of which is *Leacht var Erris*, the monument of the slaughter of Erris, near Cross, traditionally said to mark the sepulchre of a King of Munster, who was slain there in a battle with the people of Connaught. It is an irregularly pyramidal cairn, about fifteen feet in height; it lies within the remains of a nearly circular entrench-ment; there are several such cairns in the neighbourhood, one of which, on being opened, was found to contain the skeleton of a man buried in the upright position. Leacht var Erris was for a long time buried beneath the sandhills, though its name and situation, and the history of the battle were still remembered by the people; but one night early in the present century a great storm blew off the sand

---

[1] This letter is pasted inside the cover of a copy of Knight's "Erris" in the Library of the Royal Irish Academy.

and left the monument exposed, as well as a wide space round it, which was strewed with human bones. There are also the remains of an ancient cemetery, containing many graves, or cists of stone flags in the sands of Cross; these tombs are arranged in groups of three, lying parallel to one another. C. O. states that the remains in these had been burnt, as the bones were charred; polished flat stones and fragments of rings of steatite were discovered in these graves. About half a mile to the southward is another stone tomb, known as *Leacht na Calliagh*, or the hag's monument.

Some of the ruins at Inisglora were considered by O'Donovan and others to have originally been the dwellings of the aboriginal inhabitants, the Damnonii, converted in after times to monastic use. These are, three *tor-thighs*, or bee-hive shaped houses, the largest *tor-thigh mor* being 10½ feet in diameter,[1] the other about 10 feet; an artificial cave, or *uaigh*, now closed up, said to communicate with some of the other buildings; and a *caisiol* or circular-walled enclosure containing these. It would appear to have been about fifty yards in diameter. In 1838 the foundations of about fifty-six yards of this *caisiol* were traceable.[2]

The Christian antiquities, though interesting to the archæologist, are of little importance in a survey of this nature, and consequently require but slight mention.[3] They consist of ruins of churches and monasteries, crosses and wells. On the mainland of the Mullet the ruins are not of any very ancient date, the oldest probably being St. Derible's Church at Fallmore, in the immediate neighbourhood of which are her grave and her "keeve" or vat, at which two "patrons" used to be held annually, which were abolished about 1825 owing to some disorders arising out of them.[4] The other remains are the Church of Tarmoncarra, of which only a small portion of the wall remains, and Cross Abbey, a structure of comparatively modern date, having been founded posterior to 1216. "By an inquisition taken, 27th Queen Elizabeth, this monastery was found in possession of three-quarters of land, with the tithes of the same each quarter being valued at 13*s*. 4*d*. sterling annually" (Knight, p. 111).

The ecclesiastical buildings on the islands are of earlier date, the

---

[1] This is now known to the people as "St. Brendan's Cell."

[2] O'Donovan, MS. letters.

[3] For information as to these, see Lord Dunraven's "Notes on Irish Architecture."

[4] This church is fully described and illustrated in Lord Dunraven's "Notes on Irish Architecture."

oldest probably being the small oratory of St. Brendan, on Inisglora, of dry stone, and measuring twelve feet by eight internally.[1] This building contains the remains of the wooden statute of St. Brendan, long famed on this coast; it used formerly be kissed by all visitors, and miraculous powers were imputed to it; now from exposure and damp it has been reduced to a shapeless lump of decayed wood; besides this there are two churches, *Teampull na-bfear,* the church of the men, 23 feet by 10 feet, and *Teampull na-mban,* the church of the women. There are also small enclosures, supposed to be the garden of the monastic settlement, in which garlic grows wild. The island was inhabited as late as 1616 by a monk named Walsh. On North Inishkea there is an old church which was dedicated to St. Columbkille; it has a doorway of the wedge shape, and is in fairly good preservation, the islanders being very scrupulous in the care of their antiquities.

On South Inishkea the foundations of a similar building may be traced. The holy wells are those of St. Derible on Inishkea and at Fallmore, and the celebrated well of St. Brendan on Inishglora; the belief in the antifeminine qualities of this well seem to have arisen from its being inside the bonds of the monastery. Finally, there are several ancient crosses, the most curious being the incised slabs of Inishkea and Duvillane; the others are the cross of Tarmoncarra referred to in a previous section, and the monumental stone near Fallmore, known as *Leacht Mic Maithin, Ioris,* after a native of that region, whose house was at that time the most western in Connaught; he does not seem to have been distinguished for anything else.

(*b*) There have of late years been many finds of antiquities consisting chiefly of articles of ecclesiastical use, mainly in North Inishkea. Mr. J. A. Nolan, of Belmullet, has obtained in the shell mounds on Inishkea a considerable number of pins and needles of bone, bronze, and copper; some of these are of curious workmanship. He also possesses the fragments of a bowl of composition with a jet edge, found by some of the islanders, who broke it up as being a "fairy bowl." An antique bell (bronze?) was found some time ago in the ruins of St. Columbkille's Church, North Inishkea, by Phillip Lavelle, king of the island, who preserved it.

Other objects of later date have been found—a chalice of the seventeenth century, on Inishkea, a pectorial cross and pyx of silver, dated 1669, some coins, &c.[2]

---

[1] The antiquities of Inishgluair are described in "Notes on Erris."

[2] Since the above was written several querns of smaller size than any now in use have been found in some of the duns.

VII.—HISTORY.

The history of the district forms a necessary portion of a report such as this, to show what changes have occurred in the composition of the population, what elements have been imported, and their effects. Unfortunately the material for a history of Erris is both meagre and much scattered, long periods being left unaccounted for, except by vague tradition or by the fanciful conjectures of some writers.

The following sketch, though not pretending to be complete, gives an outline of what seems to be the recorded history as gathered from the few writers who have dealt with the subject.

Erris was anciently known as *Iorrus Domhnann* from its earliest recorded possessors the *Domhnanns* or Damnonii (" deep diggers "), a party of Firbolgs, who, landing at Broad Haven under the leadership of their chiefs *Genann* and *Rudhraighe*, settled the surrounding country, which they held for some centuries, together with another tribe of the same people, the Gamaradii (*Gamhraidhe Iorris*). They were first subjugated to some extent by the *Danaans*, and in the second century, were, according to the annalists, conquered and enslaved by Tuathal Teachtmar, a Milesian or Scotic monarch ; it does not appear, however, that the conquerers in either case drove out or exterminated the original population, who were probably too numerous for that, and it is even doubtful if it was permanently subjugated, as many of the old writers speak of the Belgae as being still in power in the fifth century. From this period until the year 1180, there is no record of the people. Adamnan indeed speaks of the district as Erris of the Damnonii, but does not state whether that people were still in power or no. Respecting this long silence, O'Donovan says (MS. Letters) : " I, who have felt deep interest in the history of Erris these seven years, and who have studied a great part of the "*rags and rhymes*" of history, have not yet discovered any notice of it from the period of the Belgae till the year 1180, when the Fiachrian O'Caithniadh[1] is mentioned as the chief of it.

The following are the records in the " Annals of the Four Masters " respecting this family :—

" A.D. 1180.—Aodh O'Caithniadh, lord of Iorris, was treacherously slain by O'Ceallachain at Cill Chomain."

" A.D. 1206.—Caithniadh O'Cathniadh, lord of Iorris, died."

---

[1] This name is probably modernised O'Kane.

" A.D. 1274.—Feargal O'Caithniadh, lord of Iorris, died in Hy-Mac Caichaim (near Invermore, in the north of Erris)."

These O'Caithniadhs were thus in power up to the end of the thirteenth century, after which there is no more mention made of them. They were a branch of the descendants of Fiachra, a Milesian chieftain, and Erris, during their sway, formed part of the region known as Hy Fiachrach or the O'Dowda's country. The chief seats of the O'Dowd's in Erris were *Oileach of the King's*, a fort built nearly on the spot where Bingham's Castle now stands, and Dun Caechain (now Dun Keeghan, on Broad Haven), but there is another smaller fort, Dun Fiachra in Aughadoon, north of the Mullet, traditionally said to have been another of their seats. The O'Dowda's reign came to an end, and the Barrets, Burkes, Lynnots, and other Welsh and Anglo-Norman families began to obtain a footing in the country about the beginning of the fourteenth century, and by 1386 seem to have got the sovereignty. They built several castles in the Mullet, of which the remains of only one can now be traced. Their rule was wide-spread, and many of their descendants are to be met with who still nourish the memory of their ancestors glory. The keeping and defence of Erris was given after the battle of Moyne by *William Mor na Maighare* (William the Great of Moyne)[1] the head of the Barrets, to Toimin and to Philpin, the grandson of Toimin (Duald M'Firbis). The Barrets ruled until the reign of Elizabeth, when some of their property was forfeited, as is thought by O'Donovan, who, however, states that he has no documentary proof.

In the reign of James I. one Darby Cormick bought a large part of this territory, and his descendants ruled until the reign of Charles II., when the land was forfeited. It was somewhere at or before this time that an influx of Ulster Celts into the district took place. These were mainly O'Donnels, O'Reillys, and a few others. Other parts of the district were forfeited during the commonwealth, so that when M'Firbis wrote there was neither Bourke, Barret, nor O'Dowd holding property in Erris. In the reign of Charles II. a grant was made of the whole half barony of Erris, the parish of Doonfeeny, in Tyrawley, and the parish of Tarmonbarry in the county of Roscommon to certain London citizens in charge for Sir James Shaen, Knight and Baronet. Sir Arthur Shaen, son of Sir James, introduced into Erris a Protestant colony who were mainly settled in the Mullet; they were

---

[1] This battle was fought in 1281, between the Barrets and Cusack who was assisted in the fight by two of the native Irish, Faithleach O'Boyle and Faitbleach O'Dowd; it resulted in the defeat of the Barrets.

given leases and were accompanied by a clergyman of their own persu-
asion; the only original inhabitants obtaining leases were the Cormicks.
This colony does not appear to have made any extensive change in the
composition of the population, as the settlers after a time ceased to be
agriculturists to any extent, and took the natives of the district on to
their lands as tenants. A curious petition to Sir Henry Bingham,
Governor of Connaught, in reference to the revenge taken on these
settlers by the natives, shows the names of those in the district in the
reign of Queen Anne, and of these but two now remain, all the rest
having disappeared, a fate which is ascribed by Mr. Knight to the
habits of extravagance induced by the nature of their life. Sir Arthur
Shaen began the canal across the neck of the Mullet, but soon abandoned the project, which was not revived until after the foundation of
the town of Belmullet. Sir Arthur's two daughters, he had no sons,
married, one Henry Boyle Carter of Castlemartin, county Kildare, and
the other John Bingham Esq., Newbrook, county Mayo, and the
property was divided between these two.

In the year 1793 a fight took place in the Mullet between the
local yeomanry and the people of the district, in which thirty-six of the
latter were slain. The origin of the fight was the opposition to the
enrolment of the militia, then causing a great stir in the west of
Ireland. Major Bingham having come to reside in the Mullet in 1796
built Bingham Castle at Eley, and began to make some roads and
reclaim some of the land. The first road into the district was made in
1823, and about the same period Major Bingham founded the town in
the Mullet known as Binghamstown, which at first was fairly prosper-
ous and had at one time a population of 673.

In 1823 the first vehicle entered the Mullet, and in 1824 Mr. W. H.
Carter founded the town of Belmullet at the neck of the peninsula.
This town being more favourably situated, has completely destroyed
its rival Binghamstown, which, though once containing some fine
buildings, is now in ruins, and contains only about a dozen inhabited
houses. From the time of the establishment of Belmullet and the construction of good roads into the districts, the condition of the people has
shown steady improvement, though it is still extremely primitive and
poverty-stricken.

VIII.—Concluding Remarks.

This report being, like its two predecessors, a record of available
facts, as found, in order to form a basis for comparison between different parts of the country, all advocacy of personal theories or opinions

has been carefully avoided, it being evident that in the present state of British ethnology there is not sufficient material available from which to draw exact conclusions as to what race or admixture of races forms the bulk of the population of this part of Erris. History when combined with a study of the folk-names gives some slight help in this respect. So far as records go, the population seems to have been until comparately recent times an almost unmixed one, as it does not appear as if the aboriginal inhabitants, though several times sub-dued and enslaved, had ever been driven out or exterminated. Of the immigrations into the district those having greatest effect upon the population would seem to have been that of the fifteenth and four-teenth centuries, the rule of the Barrets, Burkes, and other Walsh or Anglo-Norman families, whose surnames now bulk largely among the people, and the influx into Erris of the O'Donnells and others from Ulster in the sixteenth and seventeenth centuries.

Of these two the former would seem to have entered more largely into the composition of the people than the latter, but it should not be concluded that all those who bore the surnames of Barret, Burke, &c., were of Welsh or Anglo-Norman blood, as the followers of many of the chiefs of these names were in the habit of assuming their leaders' names, though themselves aborigines of Connaught. The descendants of the Ulster people, though to some extent settled in this district, are for the greater part a colony by themselves in the mountainous region of Ballycroy in the south of Erris.

Tne English Protestant colony introduced by Sir Arthur Shane, having almost from the first set up as small landlords or middlemen, subletting their holdings, did not mix to any extent with the original inhabitants who became their tenants, have left but few descendants, most of the families having left this part of the country. It is said that about Portacloy the people are mainly of Ulster origin, but that there has been a slight admixture of French blood from the intermar-riage amongst them of some soldiers of Humbert's forces who, escaping after their defeat at Ballinamuck, found refuge in that wild moun-tainous district.

The inhabitants of Inishkea possess, as has been before stated, quite different characters, physically and otherwise, from those of their mainland neighbours; they have no traditions as to their origin, but may be looked upon as probably the most unmixed representatives of the original inhabitants of the district.

IX.—BIBLIOGRAPHY.

The following make more or less mention of the district and the people, but this list does not profess to be exhaustive :—

ANONYMOUS.—"The Saxon in Ireland " (1851).

BALD.—"Map of the County of Mayo" (1813).

BALFOUR, MISS.—"Two Visits to the West Coast of Connaught." (Murray's Magazine, August, 1891.)

BENNETT.—"Six Weeks in Ireland" (1848).

DUNRAVEN, E.—"Notes on Irish Architecture " (edited by Margaret Stokes).

THE FOUR MASTERS (*cf.* O'DONOVAN).

KARNEY, J.—"Richard Barrett, The Bard of Mayo." (The Gaelic Journal, vol. v., p. 136, 1894.)

KNIGHT, PATRICK, C.E.—"Erris in the Irish Highlands and the Atlantic Railway." (Dublin, 1836.)

MAC FIRBIS, DUALD (*cf.* O'DONOVAN).

MAXWELL, W. H.—"Wild Sports of the West " (1832).

M'PARLAN.—"Statistical Report of County Mayo" (1801).

OCEANUS.—"Halifax N.S. to Blacksod." (Dublin, 1895.)

O'DONOVAN, JOHN :

　　"MSS. Letters to the Ordnance Survey of Ireland " (1838). Now in the Library of the Royal Irish Academy.

　　"The Annals of the Kingdom of Ireland," by the Four Masters. Translated and annotated by JOHN O'DONOVAN, LL.D.

　　"The Genealogies, Tribes, and Customs of Hy Fiachrach, commonly called O'Dowda's Country. From the Book of Lecan in the Royal Irish Academy, and from the Genealogical MS. of Duald Mac Firbis, in the Library of Lord Roden." (Dublin, 1844.)

O'FLAHERTY, R.—"Ogygia."

OFFICIAL :

　　"Census of Ireland, 1891, vol. iv., No. 3."

　　"Memoirs of the Geological Survey of Ireland." Memoir of Sheet.

C. O. (OTWAY, REV. CÆSAR).—"Sketches in Erris and Tyrawley." (Dublin, 1841.)

Society for the Preservation of the Irish Language :
"oιðe ċloιnne lιp. The Fate of the Children of Lir."
(Dublin, 1883.)

Trotter.—" Walks through Ireland."

Warren, R.—" Birds observed breeding on the coasts of Sligo and Mayo." " The Irish Naturalist," vol. iv. p. 180. (Dublin, 1895.)

Note.—The late Dean Lyons, of Kilmore, the well-known archæologist, had written the history of Erris, but died without publishing it. The ms. is now missing, but was until lately in the possession of the Rev. James Durcan of Bangor, Erris.

EXPLANATION OF PLATES.

(*From Photographs, by* C. R. & J. M. Browne.)

PLATE XV.

Fig.
1. Group of men at Muingerena, Mullet. Taken in order from left to right, the names are :—

Back row—Patrick Toole, James M'Cormack, Patrick Padden, James Dixon, No. 50; J. Lavelle.

Front row—Francis Coyle, No. 47; Hugh Cafferky, No. 46; Anthony Lavelle, No. 51; H. Joyce.

2, 3. Anthony Dunleavy, aged 60 years, Emlybeg, No. 13.

4. William Gaughan, aged 28 years, Emlybeg, No. 12.

5. —— ——, ——, No. 41; Richard Cane, No. 40. Both from Fallmore, a small village at the southern extremity of the peninsula of the Mullet.

PLATE XVI.

6. Group of men from Iniskea.

7, 7a. Michael Cawley, aged 41 years ; South Iniskea, No. 4.

8. Philip Lavelle, aged 33 years; North Iniskea, No. 1.

9, 9a. Patrick Cawley, aged 40 years ; South Iniskea, No. 3.

PLATE XVII.

10. Group of men and boys at Portacloy. The figure on the extreme right shows the dress of the younger boys.

11, 12. William Bourne, aged 33 years, No. 34, and —— Bourne, both from Portacloy.

Proc. R.I.A., Vol. 3, Ser. 3.

Plate XV.

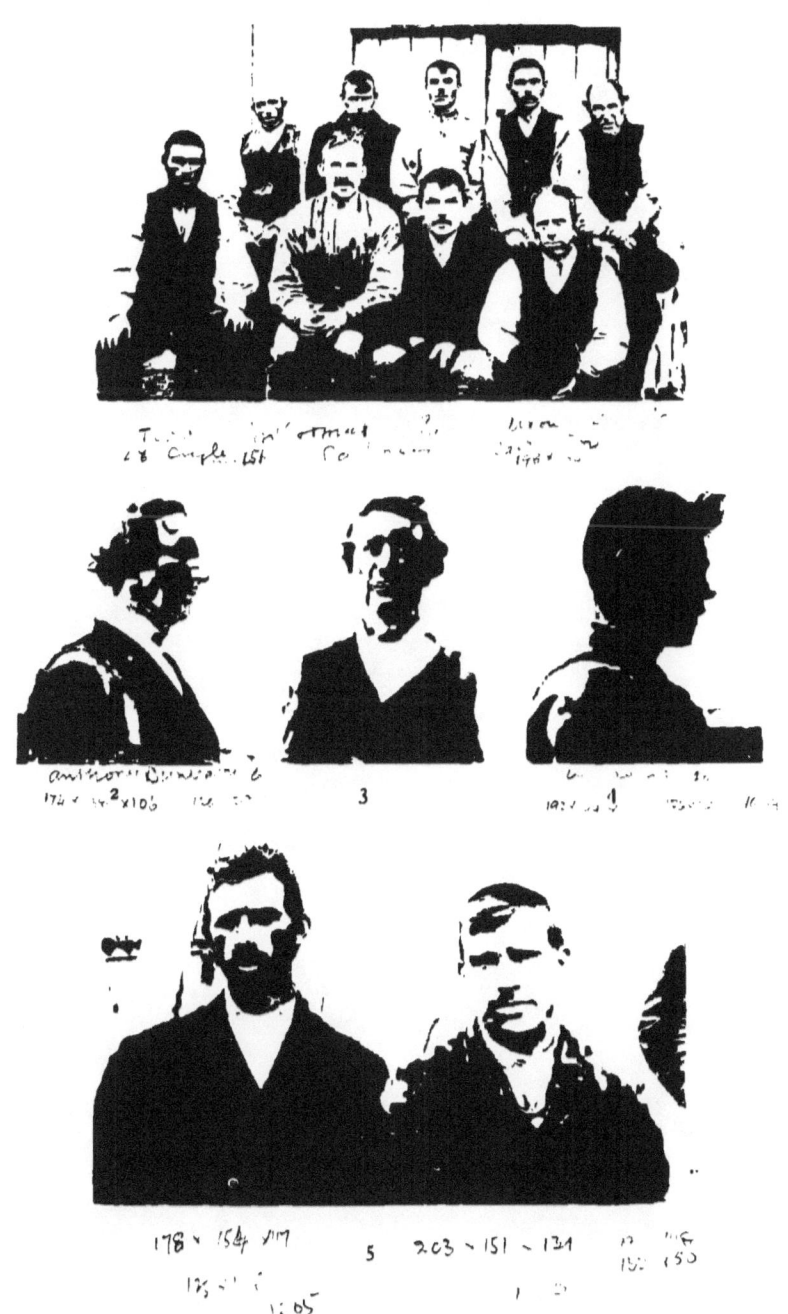

9 (a)   7 (a)

10

11

12